Charley

and the

Magic Jug

and Other Stories

Rosemary and Larry

MILD

Magic Island Literary Works • Honolulu, Hawaii • 2022

"Tsunami!" was published in *Dark Paradise: Mysteries in the Land of Aloha* (Anthology, 2017). Reprinted by permission.

Interior book design by Larry Mild.
Cover design by Larry Mild.
Library of Congress Cataloging-in-Publication Data

Mild, Rosemary P.; Mild, Larry M.
Charley and the Magic Jug and Other Stories

Mild, Rosemary P.; Mild, Larry M.

ISBN 978-0-9905472-7-3
First Edition 2022

10 9 8 7 6 5 4 3 2 1

Dedication

For our wonderful daughters—
Jackie and Myrna

For our beloved grandchildren—
Alena, Craig, Ben, Leah, and Emily

For our darling great-grandsons—
Kai and Oliver

For our marriage—soul mates, partners, lovers

My Special Tribute

The oil painting on the front cover is titled *Boy with Jug*. It was painted by my grandfather Charles Morris Glueck (1875-1955). He was born in Hungary and emigrated to the U.S. as a young adult. Grandpa told me that he copied the painting from a magazine photo, and then painted his own boyhood face instead of the original face. It is one of two paintings he did that hang in our apartment in Honolulu today. The fantasy story "Charley and the Magic Jug" is a loving tribute to Grandpa Glueck's memory.

—Larry Mild

Acknowledgments

We could fill an entire volume with the names of all the family members, dear friends, and acquaintances who are loyal fans of our books, essays, and short stories. You, our readers, are all precious to us and give us the ultimate push to continue our writing.

Our special thanks and hugs to:

Sisters in Crime/Hawai'i Chapter and Hawai'i Fiction Writers, for their friendship, encouragement, and advice.

Diane Farkas, our close friend, for her outstanding proofreading skills.

Disclaimer

Charley and the Magic Jug and Other Stories is a work of fiction. The plots and events therein are of the authors' imagination and invention. All characters are fictitious and any resemblance to persons living or dead is purely coincidental. A few real locations have been altered to accommodate the stories. Some product brand names are ficticious.

Table of Contents

"Short stories are tiny windows into other worlds and other minds and other dreams. They are journeys you can make to the far side of the universe and still be back in time for dinner."

—Neil Gaiman (on *Goodreads*)

Books Coauthored by the Milds

The Dan and Rivka Sherman Mysteries
- Death Goes Postal
- Death Takes A Mistress
- Death Steals A Holy Book
- Death Rules the Night

The Paco and Molly Mysteries
- Locks and Cream Cheese
- Hot Grudge Sunday
- Boston Scream Pie

Adventure/Thrillers
- Cry Ohana
- Honolulu Heat

Short Story Collections
- Murder, Fantasy, and Weird Tales
- The Misadventures of Slim O. Wittz
- Copper and Goldie, 13 Tails of Mystery and Suspense in Hawai‘i
- Charley and the Magic Jug and Other Stories

A Science-Fiction Novella
- Unto the Third Generation

* * * *

By Rosemary
- Miriam's World—and Mine
- Love! Laugh! Panic! Life with My Mother
- In My Next Life I'll Get It Right

By Larry
- No Place To Be But Here, My Life and Times

Charley and the Magic Jug

Rumor had it that a mysterious cave nestled deep within the Zemplén mountain range in Hungary, not far from the tiny village of Zylék. Some thought its existence was an old wives' tale, but a select few knew better. One person in particular appeared to know just where this cave might be found. It was said that a fourteen-year-old lad, Károly Glueck, could lead you directly to the entrance, but he always refused to do so. Károly claimed that he only stumbled upon the cave once while chasing a stray goat, one of his father's herd of a dozen. The boy insisted he had long since forgotten his way there, because he merely followed the mischievous goat without paying attention to its actual path.

Most of the villagers did not believe this excuse. They accused him of being selfish. Others insisted there was no such cave. But the boy had proof, although he couldn't reveal it to anybody. It was a secret, his very own secret.

Károly preferred to be called Charley; he simply liked the playful sound of this anglicized version of his given name. He learned this new name from a British tourist hiking across the Zemplén mountain range. The Brit had accepted a half-dozen days of hospitality, for rest and nourishment, at the Glueck family home, but he couldn't be bothered pronouncing Károly. He dubbed the teen Charley and the

1

name stuck thereafter. The two shared the lad's bedroom.

Early each morning Charley's dad, Csőrö, trudged up the grassy slope to the corral. He hitched the twelve goats to a rope, one after the other, and walked from door to door through the village of Zylék. At each doorstep Csőrö would milk the goats for the ladies of the house. Though the pay for goat's milk and cheese products was meager, the stoic dairyman was able to eke out a living for his family of four—his wife, their daughter, and son. When the tall, stocky herder of forty-seven years reached the last of his supply, he would return the goats to the grassy slope. Charley would meet him there and keep watch over the grazing flock while his father went home to farm a small patch of adjacent land. Charley routinely stayed with the goats until dusk, when he herded them into a wooden shed before returning home for chores. This ramshackle structure securely contained the goats overnight.

Built tall and solid like his father, Charley was both agile and strong. He had to be, tending the flocks in all sorts of weather over the rough and rugged terrain bordering the mountains. But, unlike his father, he had a dreamy, sensitive side, with soulful, copper-colored eyes; a round face with cheeks ruddy from the sun; and thick auburn hair that flopped over his forehead. Often, when the lad wasn't paying enough attention, one or more goats would wander off the grasslands and up onto the rocky ledges. Discovering that the strays were gone, Charley would then have to lead the remainder of the herd into the shed and give chase to the missing ones.

Ah, yes, the cave. A year earlier, in June of 1904, one of the goats wandered off the grasslands while Charley had his nose in a book. When the lad finally looked up, he saw the stray darting from rock to rock—hesitating here and there to snack on tempting vegetation—and climbing to higher and higher elevations. The lad herded the rest of the flock into the shed and took off after the mischievous goat, who had a considerable head start.

In order to make up time, Charley took a direct yet far more dangerous route, a precarious one he had never taken before, to recover the stray. Instead of the safe, well-worn, switchback path to higher elevations, he chose to claw over rock, sand, and briar bush. The lad was an experienced climber. However, that day each section was new, with its own hazards. Keeping track of the goat while climbing added to his difficulty. At one point nearly seventy-five meters up, he slid downward a good six meters before recovering a decent foothold. Raw fingers and thorny scratches accumulated on his bare arms and legs as he again attempted to close the gap between them. He wished he'd worn cover-up clothes instead of his usual cotton britches and sleeveless shirt. Fortunately, the goat had discovered a fat, juicy bush to gnaw on and was spending considerable time there on a narrow ledge about thirty meters above him.

When Charley finally arrived on the same outcropping, he found the goat chewing and pulling at the large, healthy bush until it bent away from the rocks. As the lad came closer, he slipped a length of rope around its leather collar. The goat, still munching away, hardly noticed. But Charley saw something curious: a wide opening in the rocks beyond the bush that would normally be hiding it. He tied the opposite end of the tether around the bush's sturdy trunk. After climbing a few more meters, he approached what appeared to be a hidden cave entrance.

The late afternoon sun cast sufficient light into the entrance for Charley to see his way inside. The cave extended inward about twenty meters. A physical jolt of excitement gripped him. He ducked into the opening. Once past the neck of the cave, he was astonished to find that he could easily stand. He whirled about in each direction, taking in all there was to see. As his eyes grew accustomed to the deep shadows, the lad was stunned to see something beyond the works of nature in this rocky structure. Three pottery jugs, maybe four liters each in size, stood on a flat, smooth rock. Each one was a different color: one rose red; one cobalt blue; and one a dull earthen tone with mustard-colored decoration.

Charley saw an inscription on the flat table rock and moved close enough to decipher what it had to say. The letters and language, Csángó or Moldavian, were local and familiar, and the message was quite clear. **"Take only one and prosper, but choose wisely, for the** choice is offered only once."

The lad knew of nothing on which to base a wise choice. He thought for a moment. The light would soon be gone, so he needed to be quick about his decision. Two of the jugs were attractive in color, and one was plain. *Perhaps the contents will tell me more. I'll sample all three.*

Charley tilted the cobalt blue jug first and poured a clear liquid into the palm of his hand. Lapping it up, he discovered pure mountain stream water. The rose jug yielded a light, sweet rosé wine of the region at the perfect temperature. The plain earthen jug surrendered goat's milk: cool, nutritious, and refreshing.

Charley pursed his full lips and squinted as he pondered, knowing the right choice was critical. *Water is plentiful in our village with so many mountain streams, so it would be hard to sell. And such a quantity of perfect wine, I'd be accused of stealing. Ah, the milk would be a welcome addition to my father's trade. He would be able to expand the number of customers he now serves. I'll take the earthen jug.*

Charley lifted the heavy jug, tucked it in the crook of his left arm, and crawled through the neck of the cave to the outside ledge. The goat had eaten its fill and now slept nearby. Dusk had settled over the sharp ledge, and darkness would cover them soon, making it too dangerous to descend until morning. The lad curled up in the neck of the cave for warmth with one arm hugging the precious jug, and didn't wake until the first crack of dawn. Then, with the tether rope in one hand and the earthen jug under the opposite arm, he started down the much easier switchback path to the grazing land below. Hurrying, it still took him more than two hours to descend to the greener level.

Arriving on the grassy slope, he discovered that his father had already strung the remaining eleven goats together in a train and was ready to head to the village. Csörö had been ready to scold his son for being out all night and for leaving him with only a herd of eleven, but when he saw all the scratches and bruises on the boy's arms and legs, his displeasure turned to compassion. The son explained his adventure to his father, and Csörö suspiciously sampled the jug's contents. He was soon convinced of their good fortune.

Charley followed him from village door to village door that day. When the last goat gave her most, his father turned to Charley's jug so he could continue to sell milk to new customers. Those who were skeptical of the milk's freshness were given a free sample. The lad and his dad continued the arrangement for a few days, fully expecting the jug to exhaust its supply at any time. It never did, so on the following morning, Charley stuck a straw down into the mouth of the jug to see how much was really left. He was surprised to find that it was nearly full, pure and sweet, with that good strong goaty flavor. Thereafter, he tested the jug every day with the same result—to his amazement a seemingly bottomless gift.

As one season followed another, the jug gradually took on a reddish, maroon tint, transforming the formerly drab earthenware into the rich colors of a glowing sunset.

It was not long before the Glueck family income tripled, and they were able to afford a few luxuries. They were even generous to their neighbors, who never questioned the family's newfound cash flow. Their generosity extended to strangers, who were never turned away. Presently, the British hiker came back to stay with them. The glib young traveler brought with him a sense of humor and stories from the outside world that fascinated the whole family.

The blond, blue-eyed Brit was handsome and athletic and fresh out of Cambridge University. His full name was Brandon Bakersfield III. Sharing a huge featherbed with Charley each night, Brandon had the opportunity to observe his young host, the lad he'd dubbed Charley. Before retiring for the night, Charley would sit on his bed in his pajamas with the large maroon jug under one arm and recite his prayers aloud. The lad was extremely possessive of this jug and even slept with it next to his bed. By day, it was always close to him, especially when he and his father went out to sell their milk. Brandon was puzzled. Although the jug was moderately attractive, he assumed it would bring only a few coins at market.

So why is it so darned precious? he wondered. *And why is this family of a mere herder and farmer able to afford so much?*

5

On the third day of his stay, Brandon decided to follow Csörö and Charley on their daily rounds with the goats and the jug. He observed nothing unusual until he saw Charley filling containers provided by the customers at successive doorsteps. On and on, door to door, the lad kept pouring. Brandon couldn't remember seeing the boy ever fill the jug. *Where and how did he fill the jug when the goats were giving their all on the village trek?* he wondered. *Where was the milk coming from?*

On days four and five, Brandon followed them again with the same result—seemingly endless milk. During all that time, his eyes never left the vibrantly colored red jug. Now he was convinced that it had magical powers. While Charley slept, Brandon even watched through the darkness of those last two nights, so there was no way the jug got filled without him seeing it.

There had always been a seed of greed lurking inside the family's guest, and Brandon could almost feel it growing inside him. *If I can just manage to get the jug back to England, I can start a dairy with hardly any financial outlay—an endless supply, and little or no overhead. The Gluecks are nice people, but they really don't know to run a business. The jug is wasted on them. Besides, there aren't enough customers out here in the sticks. I need to steal the magic jug. But how?* The jug and the boy were always inseparable. Nighttime seemed to afford the most plausible opportunity, as the hard-working lad usually slept deeply and untroubled.

On the sixth and last day of Brandon's visit, he packed up his belongings. Everyone knew he had planned to leave the following morning. He had given no one any reason to suspect his intent. He planned to take advantage of the boy that last night. The Brit's plan also included stealing Charley's bicycle as a getaway vehicle. The main road was only 150 meters down the lane. From there he would have smooth sailing. Best of all, the village had no telephone service.

Nightfall seemed slower than usual to Brandon that night, and the lad's prayers seemed excessively long. Charley usually snored when he lay on his back, but tonight he lay on his left side with his right hand wrapped around the mouth of the jug.

Brandon waited two hours, hoping the lad would shift to his back. At last he heard the snoring. The Brit slipped out of his side of the bed and pulled on his clothes. He stole around the bed to find Charley asleep on his back with his left hand gripping the jug. *They might as well be attached*, Brandon thought. He had an idea: *The chair with the lad's clothes draped across the back is just the right height.* Brandon silently moved the chair adjacent to the jug. Gently, he pried the boy's fingers off the jug. Then, lifting the lad's arm by the pajama sleeve, he transferred it to the chair cushion and let it rest there. The boy slept on, and he crept out of the house.

Before Brandon climbed onto the bicycle, he tilted the jug and splashed a tiny puddle of milk into his palm to taste the contents and prove that the jug would work for him as well. It tasted fresh, and cool, too. He stowed his nefarious prize in the bicycle basket and rode off down the lane to the main road. Still in darkness, then half the next day, he peddled all the way to the first big city that had a railroad station. There he bought a train ticket to a coastal port, where he knew he could board a passenger ship.

Three days later Brandon landed back in Sussex, England. Spending the last of his inheritance, he rented a store, purchased refrigeration machinery, acquired several milk delivery trucks, bought thousands of suitable bottles, and hired three employees. As the days of preparing to launch his new business passed, he kept sampling the milk to see if the jug was still working for him. It passed every test.

But what he failed to notice was that the jug itself was slowly reversing color—from vibrant maroon to reddish brown to ocher to the original plain earthen hue.

With great fanfare, the momentous day arrived to launch his dairy business. Early in the morning, one of his assistants began to pour from the jug—only the neck of it clogged. He called Brandon over and told him of the difficulty. Using a long, thin mixing rod, they managed to break up the clog.

What flowed out was sour, curdled, and spoiled goat's milk. Brandon decided to wash out the jug and delay the launch of his dairy venture for another day, hoping the jug would again produce a cool, clean batch. Of course, the jug denied him the next day and the one after that. On the third day the earthenware jug transformed itself into a mere pile of sandstone dust.

Brandon finally acknowledged that he had committed a great crime and would pay for it in financial ruin.

Meanwhile, back in the Glueck household, Csörö despaired over the theft of their precious jug—and Charley's bicycle. How could their guest have so betrayed the family's hospitality?

Nevertheless, Csörö continued to ply his trade with the purchase of four additional goats. Charley often thought about returning to the cave to obtain the rose-colored jug, but didn't because he remembered the warning: **"Take only one and prosper, but choose wisely, for the choice is offered only once."**

If chance can happen once, it can happen again. One sleepy day as Charley tended the herd, another wandering goat led him to the very same cave. Expecting to find only the two remaining jugs, the lad was surprised to find three. This time his choice was easy.

Death by Agreement

A crystal chandelier cast its glow on the mahogany dining table, set with three porcelain plates. Each plate held a generous slab of tiramisu, a rich Italian dessert. The layers of sponge cake were filled with whipped cream, powdered chocolate, and velvety mascarpone cheese—laced with coffee liqueur and enhanced with a hint of the finest rum. Three identical mouthwatering platefuls sat side by side, along with knives, forks, and napkins. Well, almost identical, according to the three young men seated there. An hour earlier, two of these generous slabs of tiramisu were also laced with a tasteless, odorless, painless, deadly poison. One slab remained pure, tasty, and harmless.

Each of the young men shuffled the plates repeatedly, swapping them end-to-end and center-to-either-end over a ten-minute period. While each one did the swapping and switching, the other two turned their backs so that none of these three Richman brothers could possibly know which plate held the harmless cake. The Italian definition of *tiramisu*, "Cheer me up," was filled with irony for the occasion.

This bizarre competition was not unlike the game of Three-card Monte, the notorious shell game where there can be only one winner. Of course, the prize had to be worth it, or the three brothers would not have agreed to gamble their lives on these dessert servings.

Best of all, they believed the survivor would not be declared a murderer. To share in the complicity, one brother purchased the poison, another loaded the syringe, and the third one discharged the syringe into two of the tiramisu slabs.

* * * *

The siblings' mother, the only source of reason in the house, had long since departed from her dysfunctional family, glad to be rid of her abusive husband. Raymond Lyonous Richman had devised an elaborate, sinister scheme, and forced his three sons to go along with it. Had they not agreed, all of his fortune would have gone to a charitable foundation with no family access to it at all. He was a diabolical man devoid of feeling, morals, and ethics. No love or even admiration existed among this father and any of his three sons. Is it any wonder that he was the sole author of this horrendous scheme? Raymond, a driven entrepreneur, had amassed such enormous wealth that he could not conceive of it being divided among his rightful heirs. In fact, he felt his wealth was the crown of his existence. Breaking it up, parceling it out in shares to his sons, would diminish and weaken the world's perception of his financial achievements. He wanted to create an absolute monarchical replica of himself—in only one son. He didn't care which one. He conjured up his vicious scheme based on his own warped logic. He felt that without this powerful incentive, his sons would misuse and waste his fortune. A week before his impending death, Raymond compelled his sons to sign a compliance agreement. Instead of survival of the fittest, it would be survival of the luckiest. Or would it be the cleverest? Only time would tell.

Maximillian Wells, his lawyer—a shrewd one, never off his game—had drawn up the agreement. Wells was a tough corporate counsel who had been through many a merger, sell-off, and asset-dismantling assault. He and two of his associates would attend to witness the event. Wells would act as referee and see that all of Raymond's wishes were carried out. Also in attendance would be Nathan Latimore, mortician at Hill Haven Mortuary. He would be in charge of the funerals and interments.

At the time of the agreement, the lives of Raymond's three

sons were in varying stages of disarray. Zachary was divorced and bored with his job as an insurance actuary. Andrew, stuck in a bad marriage, was a shady, penny-ante stockbroker, currently under investigation for personal misuse of client funds. Barton, a complete social failure with ladies and even guys, worked as a bookkeeper for a furniture chain. The brothers, all in their thirties, thoroughly disliked one another. They had grown up in an atmosphere of competition fostered by their father. Instead of teaching them loving kindness, Raymond had pitted them against each other. Notably, this was the first time they had come together to agree on anything.

* * * *

Today the agreed-to terms were to be faithfully carried out. All three brothers wore somber business suits with conservative ties— Zachary in blue herringbone, Andrew in charcoal gray, and Barton in black. There were no pleasantries beforehand. Silently, the brothers reached for the tiramisu plates in their final array—one plate clearly in front of each of them. Two brothers almost chose the same plate, but ultimately, they relented and chose their aligned portion. Fork cut by fork cut, they slowly nibbled at the delectable dessert, hoping for an indication that one or both of the others would show signs first. But the poison had been carefully timed to avoid such a revelation. Oh, yes, there were three handwritten suicide notes, one alongside each place setting.

When only crumbs were left, they looked at each other inquiringly, anticipating the deciding result. After nearly thirty minutes of waiting, Andrew's head dropped down to his chest; then his whole body slumped. Two minutes later, Barton followed suit. Each of the two wore a peaceful smile. Only one of the brothers left the table, and he felt neither guilt nor remorse. He quietly picked up his suicide note and pocketed it.

According to their plan, mortician Nathan Latimore and his assistants stood at the ready to handle the remains. Latimore, with two years of medical school under his belt, had been elected coroner of Panther County two years earlier. So, even though the two deaths weren't exactly natural, he knew exactly what had happened here and deemed there would be neither an autopsy nor a coroner's inquest. On the following Tuesday, he delivered the joint funeral service for Barton and Andrew. Nathan also furnished Max Wells with the necessary documents: two death certificates and two death notices for the *Panther County Journal*.

Meanwhile, the surviving brother, Zachary, had business to conduct at Richman Industries' corporate headquarters. Zach had an angular face and hawkish nose, bony but wide shoulders, and a confident stride. Arriving at his father's opulent office the next day, he found two detectives waiting— to arrest him for murdering his brothers. Max Wells had reported him as the sole survivor of two suspicious deaths. The detectives claimed that Zach had motive, means, and opportunity, all the evidence they needed to implicate him in the crimes.

In response, Zach produced the compliance agreement that his father had forced him and his siblings to sign. "See?" he said. "My brothers knew what they were getting into. There's no crime here, just a double suicide by Bart and Andy. How can I be held responsible for their deaths?"

Detective Greg Wilson responded. "The coroner tells us they were both poisoned. Someone had to put the poison in their desserts and that's murder in my book."

Seething inside, but determined not to cave under pressure, Zach said, "What if I told you that I was the one who purchased the poison? But it was Bart who filled the syringe, and Andy who injected it into the tiramisu."

"Can you prove that's what actually happened?" asked Greg.

"Absolutely," said Zach. "Ask the witnesses. You can't prove I had *anything* to do with my brothers' deaths."

The detective smirked, "We'll see about that. But one thing is certain. At the very least, you are somehow involved in a *conspiracy* to commit murder, and I'll prove that much, too."

Zach's gray eyes turned steely. "Detective, I'm afraid any conspiracy you can come up with has to be blamed on my father. But as you know, he's already dead."

"*Conceiving* a conspiracy to commit murder may not be unlawful in itself," said Greg. "But taking part in the execution of such a conspiracy is another thing. I think you were even compensated to participate in this conspiracy."

"I wasn't promised pay or compensation in any way," declared Zach. "I merely benefited from a highly risky wager in which I also could have paid the ultimate price. It's only by chance that I stand before you today. A wager in which all parties participate willingly cannot be construed as a conspiracy. I suggest that's something even Counselor Max Wells would agree to."

"Let me point out, sir, that you are the sole heir to your father's huge fortune," said Greg. "Max Wells is the one who drew attention to your implication in all this. Why would *he* do this? What motive could he have?"

Zach's mustache twitched as his face turned dark. "Max Wells is a rat. The SOB is betraying the last wishes of my father, his trusting client. Max had the same motive all attorneys have—to go to court and draw out the legal proceedings indefinitely. His legal fees, coming from the estate, would grow immensely, of course. Remember, he's the one who drew up the agreement. If there were any conspiracy here, wouldn't *he* be culpable as well? If he, the legal authority, thought there was anything wrong with it, would he have executed the document in the first place?"

"I suppose not," said Greg. "What I do know is that the level of this discussion has gotten way beyond my pay grade. I'm going to have to defer to the District Attorney for his wisdom."

* * * *

A month later, Zach still wondered what charges Wells and the District Attorney would come up with. He was astounded when the letter arrived stating that there would be no charges filed. The original compliance agreement, while utterly distasteful, was declared absolutely legal. This was the District Attorney's final decision. At this point, Zach wondered what part Wells had played in the DA's final assessment. After all, they were social friends.

Zach felt an oppressive load had been lifted from his back.

In the coming months, he opened four safety deposit box accounts, all in the same bank, under fictional names. He closed all of Raymond's bank accounts and divided the resulting cash equally among the boxes. As sole owner of Richman Industries, he appointed his top manager to run the firm for him—a *yes* man, to be sure. Through this manager, Zach siphoned off large chunks of the company's cash by selling many questionable assets. Again, he divided the proceeds among the four safety deposit boxes. He also declared himself a huge dividend every six months. The firm prospered, although it never seemed to grow again because of the generous semiannual dividends it declared.

When a little more than a year had passed, Zach slowly began to collect marketable gems, those that could be easily converted to cash anywhere in the world. Three of the safety deposit boxes were soon filled with gems as the cash to pay for them dwindled. At the end of the second year, he packaged up the contents of two of the boxes and sent one to A.L. Remerez in Sao Paolo, Brazil, and the other to B.L. Sanchez in Quito, Ecuador. The third box and its contents he kept for himself. The fourth box and its contents belonged to Nate Latimore; Zach had given him a duplicate key.

Zach continued to remember his living—yes, very much alive—brothers Andrew and Bart this way every year for the next four decades. His brothers were enjoying leisurely lives in South America, more or less incognito.

The injected "poison" wasn't poison after all. Bart had substituted a knockout drug for it, and Andrew had injected it into the tiramisu. The elaborate plan, devised by Zach and carried out by Nate Latimore, the wily mortician, enriched all four conspirators immensely.

Best of all, it foiled the malicious bequests of one evil old man.

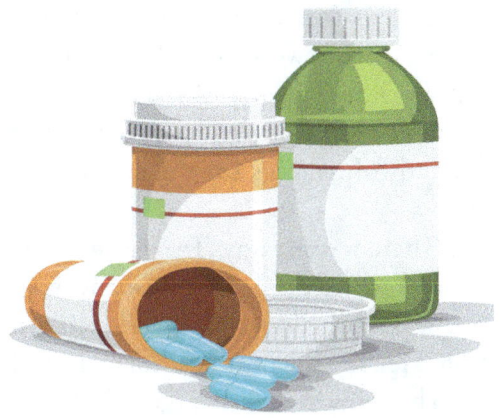

A Hard Act to Swallow

Who could foresee that something as tiny as a tasteless, palatable pill would cause marital turmoil and the upheaval of a multinational corporation? You doubt that? Oh, yes, it was the power of an isolated capsule, a mere two centimeters long by half a centimeter in diameter and weighing far less than an ounce, that caused all this misery. The story of the little turquoise pill began southwest of Akron, Ohio, in a small, blue-collar town called Curiosity.

Bradley Ainsworth and Graham Mason were equal partners in Masworth Industries, a small pharmaceutical firm. They held a strong market share in three popular prescription drugs, with patents pending on two more. In their mid-fifties and, for the most part, healthy, the two men were worth fifteen million dollars apiece. Both were shrewd businessmen and each held a doctoral degree in biochemistry.

Their wives, Cricket Ainsworth and Trish Mason, despised one another and rebelled against any social interaction. Each saw the worst of herself in the other: jealous, grasping, competitive. The mutual animosity made no sense to their husbands, who had given up trying to get them to "play nice." Both women were attractive in their own way. Cricket, a golf and tennis player, had a lean athlete's build and a blonde, carefree pixie haircut. Trish had a soft, sensual body and fluffy dark hair that caressed her neck with crinkly curls. Both in their late forties, the two women had more in common than they would admit. Both had been indifferent to obtaining a college degree and were obsessively eager to spend their husbands' wealth on gems, clothes, and furnishings for the echoing halls of their unmodest mansions.

Children? There weren't any. The Ainsworths wouldn't; the Masons couldn't; and neither wife nor husband would admit who was at fault. In any case, birthing, or even adopting, appeared to be out of the question. Heirs to the multimillions? The wives, with a few favorite charities to be showered with large gifts.

The *status quo* would have remained *quo* had Brad not run into Trish one Friday in July during cocktail hour. In the restaurant at the Fairgreen Country Club, only one table remained empty, out on the breezy veranda. The two members, unaware of the other's presence, headed straight for it from opposite directions. Standing at the wrought-iron table with its glass top, they first acknowledged each other with a haphazard greeting, then clumsily agreed to share the table without any social interaction.

This arrangement worked fine until the waitress took their orders. How could Brad *not* tell the waitress to put the drinks on *his* tab? And when a gust of wind blew Trish's napkin in his direction, his hand flew out to stop it, and her hand leaped out, incidentally landing on his hand. That simple touch brought their eyes and hands together, locked quietly for several moments. Never before had they given each other any personal thought, although he'd undressed her in his mind a number of times from a distance. But he did that with most women since he'd banished Cricket to a separate bedroom for her rampant infidelities. Her devotion to athletics had turned out to be devotion to the golf and tennis pros as well as her Pilates instructor.

Never before had Brad acted on his impulsive fantasies. He didn't believe in cheating. This encounter in the restaurant was no different. Or was it? Brad felt an icy chill splash through his nervous system. He shuddered involuntarily and wondered whether she had noticed.

Yes, she had. As if really seeing him for the first time, she noticed his neatly cut sandy hair, his sincere, sensitive look, and his open-necked shirt showing a hint of sandy chest hair. Trish felt a moist warmth in her most neglected parts. She puckered her lips and squirmed in her chair. Did he perceive her discomfort?

As a matter of fact, they both realized that alluring messages had been silently transmitted and received across the table. The two broke contact only when the waitress set their dry martinis before them. When they clinked glasses with a murmured "Cheers" and brought them to their lips, their eyes again locked in wordless communication. Its meaning became clear. Brad took her hand under the table and Trish squeezed it tightly. With all doubt removed, he slid out from his chair and she followed at a respectable distance to the front door, and then to the parking lot and his blue BMW sports coupe. This chance encounter led to the first of their many trysts at the Montrose Inn and Suites.

At first it was just for the clandestine sex. Then it became a pleasurable habit. Before long, they became addicted to one another, discovering lasting enjoyment, companionship, and love. Only then did the two yearn for other marital arrangements, more permanent measures. Brad believed Cricket wouldn't be a problem. She had often threatened him with divorce. And how many of her extracurricular activities could he actually prove? She would set a price, though, and he could easily manage that.

Trish faced a quite different situation. "Hamm," as she liked to call Graham, was a devout Catholic. She knew he would not grant her a divorce under any conditions. To him marriage was a holy contract not to be broken. Besides, he hated sex; he even thought it was dirty. He had performed his holy duty and consummated his marriage while he thought they could still procreate, but shied vehemently away from it when he learned that he was not only sterile, but impotent. Despite Trish's extreme frustration, she tolerated her husband and his neurotic attitude because he provided her with an affluence beyond her wildest needs. Sure, she had her share of fantasies, but always stayed within the limits of accepted propriety.

Brad and Trish were tired of sneaking around, so continuing in this manner wasn't acceptable. There was no telling how many of their trysts ended with deliberations on how to free themselves to marry. Many of these ideas fizzled with neither one taking any action, but the thought stuck. Hamm remained the sole obstacle.

Eventually, the discussions turned contentious, more serious, and even ugly. Soft, seductive Trish caught Brad unawares with a drastic solution: murder. He wondered, *Is that what she had in mind all along?* He felt ambushed. "Trish, that's crazy. Why don't you just get a lawyer and file for a legal separation? Then we won't have to sneak around anymore."

Her dark lashes fluttered and she adopted an appealing little-girl pout. "Hamm won't allow it. There's no other way. Darling, I love you so much. I can't bear the thought of not being with you always."

Brad brooded in silence for a few minutes. The thought of losing her charming laugh, her scent, her touch, her skills in bed overpowered him. He surrendered.

Once the concept of murder was out in the open, it was a matter of devising a clever plan. Who knew how many more trysts it took to analyze the various schemes? Trish wanted to poison Hamm, but didn't know how. She still had some reserved feelings for her husband, so she didn't want him to suffer. She wanted a poison that would make him die peacefully in his sleep, so it would look like an ordinary heart attack. After all, he was already taking Troupoxare, a little turquoise capsule targeted to atrial fibrillation.

She nuzzled up to Brad and stroked his neck. "Darling," she cooed, "can't you come up with a drug that would be an appropriate substitute for Troupoxare? And find a neat way to administer it, of course."

Now in his element, Brad was only too happy to comply. He knew of several drugs in his pharmaceutical firm's inventory that might work, but selected Monopoxare for its chemically structural similarities to Troupoxare. A forensic tox screen could hardly differentiate between the two and, over a short period of time, both would decompose and eventually disappear from the body.

The plot was born. Brad asked Trish to furnish him with one of Hamm's own capsules, so the poison would be undetectable in the prescription bottle. He also told Trish to let him know the number of once-a-day pills left in the bottle.

At ten o'clock one night, Brad waited until he was certain that all his company employees and executives had left the plant. Tapping in the laboratory door's security code, he strode to the farthest reaches of the assembly lab. There he donned a white coat and latex gloves, partly as a precaution to make himself look legitimate in case a researcher returned to tackle unfinished work. With confidence and skill, Brad proceeded. Taking the single capsule Trish had given him, he emptied out the Troupoxare and flushed the powder down the sink. After washing and drying the empty capsule, he packed it with a lethal dose of Monopoxare.

The following afternoon, the lovers met at their usual trysting place, the Montrose Inn and Suites. Brad pulled a tiny pillbox out of his jacket pocket and held it out to her. Triumphantly, he explained how he had carried out the first phase of their plot. "You're up next, babe," he said.

Trish's reaction startled him. "The rest of the plan is up to me?" A deep flush surged from her neck to her cheeks. Her breathing grew shallow and her voice quavered with anxiety. "I've changed my mind. I can't go through with it."

Brad's face turned stormy. His steely gray eyes bore into hers. "You put me through this for nothing? Let me remind you that the whole thing was your idea."

Trish's voice quavered, "I know, but I see now that it's not foolproof like I thought it was. Hamm is only fifty-five and his medication is supposed to prevent heart attacks. The police will accuse me right away. Isn't the spouse always the primary suspect? They'll be sure to find out about our love affair. The desk clerk here is always friendly, but who knows what he's thinking. Why do a husband and wife have to meet in a motel? Won't the police construe our affair as a motive for murder? As a conspiracy to commit murder? Isn't that cause for the death penalty, or life imprisonment at the very least?"

"The last execution in this state was in 2008," Brad retorted.

"Oh, well, it's okay then," Trish snapped. "Brad, we have to ditch the plan."

At that point, Brad knew he'd better lapse back into his gentler, more persuasive self. He took her by the hand, led her to the love seat, and pulled her down next to him. "Dearest," he said, his bass voice soothing. "You're worried for nothing. I've got a surprise for you." From his breast pocket he withdrew two round-trip plane tickets. He quietly explained that Trish's was for her to visit Aunt Kate in Miami Beach for eighteen days. His was for a two-week pharmaceutical conference in Reno and a college reunion in San Francisco for a total of twenty-one days. "These trips will be our airtight alibis. We'll leave in five days."

Trish laid her curly head on his shoulder and began breathing normally. Now it all sounded logical. Soon she straightened up and began calculating. "Let's see. I've checked Hamm's pill bottle. If we leave in five days there will only be sixteen pills left in the bottle. I'll slip the special pill in it that morning."

"Excellent!" Brad assured her. "The crisis will occur while we're away."

"We'll definitely be above suspicion."

The plot was executed with the required precision. Trish took pains to be extra-sweet to Hamm during the following four days, serving him delicious gourmet meals and studiously watching his favorite TV shows with him.

She returned from her trip to Florida on the nineteenth day, on schedule. But as she entered the house, she received a shock with the impact of a lightning bolt. She found a robust Hamm sitting in the den, reading the *Curiosity Register*. He looked up from his paper and muttered a cold "Hello." After her four days of lovingly fussing over him, he was angry that she'd left him alone for so long. He responded to her cheerful but cautious questions with evasive grunts.

She understood and couldn't exactly blame him. All she could do was play the attentive wife until her lover returned. But when Brad arrived back in town, he too was stunned to learn that Hamm was still walking around, alive and well. There didn't seem to be any explanation. Two days later, Trish called Brad. Nearly hysterical, she blurted out, "I just went into Hamm's room to wake him up. He's lying in bed—dead! Brad, what should I do?"

"Stay calm and call the doctor. If he thinks there's anything suspicious, he'll call the police. Don't panic. The police will conclude that it was a natural death, especially if the empty pill bottle is beside the bed. You have nothing to worry about."

"Brad, you don't understand!" she shrieked. "The pill bottle is here, but it still has twelve pills in it!"

"What the hell?" he shouted. "How is that possible?"

Trish had the answer. When she called the doctor from her dead husband's bedside, she learned that while she was away, Hamm had been hospitalized for twelve days for an abnormal fibrillation. His medication had come from the hospital dispensary during his stay. "It makes sense, doesn't it, the twelve pills still in the bottle?"

Brad's response was far from comforting. "For God's sake, Trish, we're not out of the woods. What if the poisoned pill is still in the bottle?"

Trish nearly choked at his logic. As it turned out, Brad was right. They had plenty to worry about. Because twelve pills remained in the bottle, the medical examiner decided to send them out for tox screen analysis. The poisoned pill was discovered and a police investigation began.

Detective Dexter Price caught the case. During interrogation, Trish caved first. She dramatically pointed out that, as co-owner of the pharmaceutical company, Brad had the expertise to doctor the pill. Of course, Brad turned on her. He told the detective that Trish dreamed up the whole plot. The lovers were indicted on charges of attempted murder and conspiracy to commit murder. The charge of murder itself was off the table because Hamm had died of heart disease. Trish wound up with the shorter sentence, three to five years. Brad received five to seven years because he concocted the pill.

The embittered couple never resumed their relationship after they were released. While Brad was in prison, the running of the pharmaceutical firm fell to Cricket. She sold many of its assets, including the drug patents. After withdrawing all of the firm's available cash, she bought a beach bungalow on a Caribbean island. Without leadership, patents, and adequate cash flow, the company went bust in six months.

Shortly thereafter, Cricket's newest lover, her surfing instructor, bilked her out of a small fortune and left her to a life of waitressing in a sleazy island lounge.

The Matching Years

Jared Purdy and his wife, Lily, ran the Purdy Print Shop on the east end of Second Street in Gainsburg, Pennsylvania. Their sixteen-year-old son, Donny, helped out every day after school. Calendars were their specialty, so the print shop kept particularly busy every July when they were printed well in advance of the new year.

Jared liked to tell all his customers: "There's something downright magical about calendars. If you go back every so many years, you find an identical calendar year matching the current calendar year. I mean every single month starts with a matching day of the week in each of those two separated years. I figure they're mysteriously connected somehow. Most cases, those years are either six or eleven years apart. Sometimes, they're five or twelve years apart, but that's kind of rare. And leap years? That's a whole other thing. The identical leap ones are mostly twenty-eight years apart. I don't know how they figure all this stuff out, but in my business, all I gotta do is go back and change the year numbers on the old matching calendar to correspond with the upcoming year. Then I plug in the new pictures and *voila*—you have next year's calendar ready to print. Lucky for me, it's all on the computer now."

Today, September 6th, 2016, a Tuesday, Jared and his wife were in the pressroom setting up a new run of posters for the Third

Baptist Church spaghetti supper. Lily was typing computer text and Jared was replenishing toner in one of the larger commercial printers. The doorbell tinkled. Lily called out, "Be with you in a second."

"It's just me, Ma," Donny yelled back. "Don't get up."

"Did you pick up the pictures from Mr. Ellis?"

"Sure did, and he bought me a can of cola from the vending machine while I waited. He said there are twelve new car photos on the CD—one for each month." Donny set the compact disk in its jewel case down on the table next to her.

"He's such a nice man and a good customer, too," said his mother.

Donny slipped his bookbag off his shoulders and hand-carried it to the stairs leading to the apartment above the shop.

"Lousy homework," he complained.

"Then get to it," his father called from the sink, washing spilt black toner powder from his hands.

"On it, Dad."

Lily took the CD out of its jewel case and slipped it into the computer's open slot. She brought up both the picture files and the calendar-template program from the prior matching-years' calendar. Consulting her penciled notes, she popped each sparkling new car picture into its appropriate month's page frame. When she had finished inserting the December picture, she returned to January to check the copy. It was there that she discovered her big mistake: the date at the top was still 2006, the previous matching calendar year, instead of 2017, the coming year. However, a distracting phone call led her to neglect changing the calendar year to 2017. She caught that crucial mistake only after the first completed calendar was printed, assembled, and bound. Lily set the bad one aside on a nearby shelf, intending to destroy it later. She made the final corrections, and then ran the bulk lot of the 2017 calendars through to fruition. She left the cartons open overnight for the multicolored toners to air dry.

On his way to school the next morning, Donny saw the errant calendar on the shelf, but did not notice the date, and tossed it in one of the open calendar cartons waiting to be delivered to Mr.

Edward Ellis at Ellis Motors. An hour afterward, Jared sealed the cartons and loaded them into his white panel truck. He completed the delivery and returned to the shop forty-five minutes later.

* * * *

Marty Lawson flipped burgers at Wympy's Beef Haven two blocks from Ellis Motors. A roly-poly guy in his early twenties, he had a passion for new cars even though he couldn't begin to afford one. So, on his way to and from Wympy's, he'd stop off at the dealership and give the once-over to any new vehicle on the showroom floor. Today, Marty picked up one of the new calendars, carried it home, and placed it in a kitchen drawer until the following January.

Usually, Ed Ellis was a generous man and tolerated Marty's many innocuous incursions, and the sales crew followed Ed's lead. But today Ed started to bolt toward Marty when he saw him snitch one of the calendars he'd just placed in the rack by the door for his customers. He halted a few steps later, deciding, *Reproaching him might lead to bad public relations. I'll look cheap.*

* * * *

On January 2nd, Marty hung up his new calendar in place of the old one hanging on the inside of the bathroom door. The next day, while answering a call to nature, he stared at the picture of a Cadillac convertible with its shiny red skin and sleek lines. The harder he looked, the more he was drawn into the picture and the calendar itself. It was almost magical. Never mind the *almost* part. He was literally transported to another era—so abruptly that he could hardly remember to pull his pants up.

Feeling totally frustrated and frightened, Marty walked the streets wondering, *Where am I? What am I doing here?* That is, until he recognized that he was still in Gainsburg. Only it seemed to be the Gainsburg of another period, a time some years earlier. He was almost sure that was the case, only he just had to prove it. He noticed a crumpled newspaper stuffed in a wire-mesh trash can at the curb. With plump fingers, he extracted and flattened out the paper until he saw the *Gainsburg Bugler* masthead with the date 2006. Now he was really bewildered. *How could this be? Is it some kind of magic? Or a huge joke being played on me? What the devil could have caused this? And if it's true, how in hell will I ever get back to 2017? I have to be sure I'm not trapped in a never-ending nightmare.*

Marty checked his watch. It matched the clock time on the bank building across the street. His heart quickened. *Ah, the First Gainsburg Banking and Trust Company will be able to verify the date for me.* He crossed the street, entered the bank's lobby, and approached a tall counter that served as a temporary desk for customers. Marty noted that all the deposit slips were dated 2006. He was now convinced that he'd been transported to another era. It wasn't his imagination. But wait. A small paper calendar on a folded cardboard stand presented him with the year 2017. He picked up the calendar. Holding it just inches from his face, he stared at it in disbelief. He couldn't take his eyes away from it. He stared at it until he suddenly realized he was actually seeing the page-size calendar on his own bathroom door while seated on the throne fully attired in his jeans and flannel shirt.

Was I dreaming? Marty wondered. *Did I really transport myself back and forth between 2006 and 2017 at will? Those two years are identical in their days and months. The only difference is the year. If I stare at this calendar on my bathroom door, can I transport myself back to 2006 again? There are so many questions I need to answer. Are the two calendars magical? Or am I delusional, losing my mind, turning into a schizophrenic?*

Marty shivered at the prospect of spending the rest of his life in a mental institution. But such a negative idea didn't last. He had to find out the truth. He stared and stared at the calendar on the bathroom door. And there he was, back in 2006 on the streets of Gainsburg. Again and again he transported himself through time at will. But who could he tell? Who would even believe him? He thought for a few minutes. *Willy the Wiser might believe me.*

His good friend, born William Wise, had a scheme to fit almost any situation—a way to make lots of money out of any opportunity with minimal effort. He was nicknamed Willy the Wiser by cynics who knew him. Willy often shared his scheme ideas with

Marty before he carried them out. To the naïve young Marty, the planning and presentation of each venture sounded precise, impeccable. But Willy's best intentions always led to failure, due to some unexpected flaw in the details.

Marty stubbornly continued to have faith in his friend, but the reverse was not always true. So Marty had to take Willy on a trio of round-trips through time to actually convince him. It was on that third round-trip that Willy came up with his master plan.

"Here's what we'll do. This year, 2017, we'll rob the First Gainsburg Banking and Trust Company. Right away we'll escape back to 2006 with the money. The authorities will never be able to locate us. We'll have eleven years for 2017 to roll around again—plenty of time for us to be in hiding and living different lives. The scheme is foolproof. No one will be harmed. The insurance company will reimburse the bank."

Willy's masterful scheme would take them only a few minutes to execute before they escaped via the calendar to 2006. He would take Marty's bathroom calendar with them to the bank. His plan also included a threatening note that they would hand to a teller and a toy gun.

It all sounded so logical to Marty that he agreed to it. After all, he was tired of flipping burgers for minimum wage.

Two weeks later, the robbery went off without a hitch or injury, and each man filled his own bag with loot from the teller. Staring at the 2017 calendar, the two made it back to 2006 safely, well before the law arrived on the scene. It was scary winding up in front of same bank they had just held up, but no one there in 2006 could possibly know about a robbery that would take place in 2017, eleven years afterward. In any case, the two robbers didn't feel comfortable until they had arrived at the suite they had reserved in a luxury hotel.

They sat on the twin beds, each one greedily imagining what his own share of the loot might do for him. They were so pleased with themselves that they ordered room service. When it came time to tip the waiter, Willy reached into their money bag and blinked.

Huh? He had pulled out a blank piece of paper the size of a dollar bill. When the waiter looked to Marty for a tip, the same thing happened.

The two humiliated thieves suddenly realized that all of the bills they'd stolen wouldn't be printed until sometime in the next eleven years! Marty scrounged through his jeans pockets and handed the waiter his last three legitimate singles. The disgruntled waiter slammed the door on his way out. Neither Marty nor Willy could figure out why even the cut paper blanks were in the bags—the paper should have been in either rolls or sheets as well. Perhaps it was another magical trick of the calendars—one meant to punish them for offending the years.

Now, in 2006, they were jobless and penniless. They knew that if they dared to transport themselves to 2017 they would undoubtedly be caught and end up with long prison terms.

What will happen to them? Only the pages torn off the calendar will dare tell.

Tsunami!

Suzanne Lumi's boss didn't much care for her. He didn't like her attitude—free-spirited and flamboyant. Or maybe it was the color of her eyes. One blue, one green, turning murky dark or sparkly light with her chameleon-like moods.

One thing was for sure. Editor-in-Chief Bart Gordon had never before seen Suzanne's body art, because this was the first day she'd worn a miniskirt and blouse instead of her usual pants suit. Her exotic tattoo was a jungle scene, portraying forest-green ferns and vines that traveled up her left shin from ankle to knee.

She didn't have to wait long for his reaction. Bart came stomping down the aisle to pick up the article she'd just finished writing. He lurched to a stop, his eyes fixed on her bare left leg, boldly displayed in the aisle for his benefit.

"What in blue blazes is that?"

"It's my tattoo," she said, beaming.

"I can see that, you ninny, but a jungle? And a cat's head peering out?"

"So glad you noticed. It's a memorial to my darling pussycat, Fanny, whom I had for twenty years. Isn't it marvelous? It's in the stylized manner of the French artist Henri Rousseau."

Bart suppressed a shiver. The orange tabby's amber eyes

glared straight at him. "And I thought I'd seen it all," he mumbled. He grabbed the article from Suzanne's outstretched hand and retreated up the aisle to his office.

Suzanne Lumi worked as a reporter for a popular weekly tabloid that focused on off-beat features and current news. This week's cover story was an update on a crime spree that had begun two years earlier: a string of twenty-eight successful residential burglaries. The unsolved crimes had the Honolulu Police Department totally baffled. And embarrassed. The thief, or thieves, had left nary a clue, apparently making no stupid mistakes, just disappearing into the void, except for a calling card of thoroughness. No cases of breaking-and-entering, no confrontations with homeowners or renters, and most remarkable, no violence.

The burglaries affected affluent neighborhoods on the island of O'ahu, mostly on the North Shore. The *modus operandi* was always subtle and clever. In each case, the thief preyed on residences—always with no one inside the house, where there were obvious indications of inattention and carelessness. Windows wide open with screens just begging to be easily removed. A trellis leading up to an open window on the second floor. A back door left ajar and a purse or wallet sitting on the kitchen counter—often while an unsuspecting dweller tended her front-yard garden of hibiscus and torch ginger.

* * * *

It was already after hours for Suzanne. At age twenty-five, she was a disgruntled employee, first-rate at her job, but underpaid. Running a comb through her jet-black, bowl-cut hair, she smoothed the straight bangs that marched across her high forehead. Slinging her purse strap over one shoulder, she took the stairs down to the garage. Her canary-yellow Mini Cooper revved up with a welcoming hum and rolled out onto Honolulu's downtown streets—headed for the Pali Highway. Navigating all the rush-hour traffic lights, Suzanne felt a virtual high leaving the city behind. The Pali—"cliff" in Hawaiian—cut straight through the forested Ko'olau mountain range, emerging on the salty, windward side of O'ahu. Veering left, she entered the Kamehameha Highway, feeling the exhilaration of the Pacific Ocean on her right, leading to her tiny abode on the North Shore.

The beach cottage stood on four-foot pilings and couldn't have been closer to the sea. The average high tide left only ten feet of coarse wet sand between her splintering wooden lanai and the unpredictable waves. House-hunting five years ago, all Suzanne needed to fall in love with this idyllic bungalow was one blazing sunset over the ocean. She swooped down and bought her precious home. "Needs work, but a real bargain," the real estate agent assured her. Single story, one bedroom, with a combined living room and kitchenette, and crawl-space attic. For now, she didn't need more.

But the beach that fronted her little white cottage hadn't always been so skinny. Erosion had taken its toll. Maybe one day she'd get around to doing something about it.

Zipping into the short gravel driveway, she climbed out of her car and waved to her next-door neighbor. White-whiskered Mr. Makamura sat on his near-perfect lawn, carefully pulling weeds. Suzanne hurried from the Mini to the house. At the fridge she drained a full glass of POG, her favorite pineapple-orange-guava drink. In the bedroom she changed into her running shorts and tank top, and headed outdoors once more.

Mr. Makamura was still sitting cross-legged on the grass. "Missy Lumi," he called as she trotted close by. "You hear? Thieves sneak into Miz Hing's place las night. Dey bad, take all good jewelry and son's laptop, too."

"No, I hadn't heard," Suzanne said, slowing to an in-place jog. "That's a shame, but it could have been worse, couldn't it? Audrey Hing can afford it. She's a rich woman. You and I don't have to worry so much about getting robbed. We haven't anything worth stealing." Chuckling, she waved goodbye and added forward motion to her jog on the running path.

"Mebbe you right, Missy, but stealing wrong—needs punish," he called after her.

The jogging path ran parallel to a community access road, then a tall hedgerow, and beyond it, the Kam highway. Cottages and two-story vacation rentals were scattered between the running path and the beach. Set comfortably back, at varying distances and higher levels, were the much more substantial, even elegant, homes that sold for around three million. Many featured stone seawalls and tough vegetation as buffers against the ocean.

Along her jogging route, Suzanne encountered Bjorn Pettersen, seated in a lawn chair in front of his rented cottage. Heavy-metal rock blared from his boom box. As he applied wax to his surfboard, his right hand moved vigorously back and forth, almost in time to the beat.

Suzanne sang out to him, "That looks like *beaucoup* elbow grease just to surf a wee bit faster. Is it worth it?"

"What's that?" he yelled back after squelching the music.

She repeated her question, but louder, interrupting her run to trudge through tall grasses.

"Sure it's worth it, Suzy. What's new, kiddo?"

"Nothing, really. Just another workday with my new boss."

"Say, did you hear about that earthquake just off of Honshu, Japan?" asked Bjorn.

"Yeah. Saw it on the news wire," she replied. "Rattled a bunch of tall buildings, lots of flooding, casualties, too." When Bjorn returned to his jar of wax, she said, "Take care now" and trotted back to the running path.

A mile later, Hetty Burger called out to her from her lanai, where she was sweeping wind-blown sand off the flooring. As Suzanne slowed to a stop, she noticed Hetty's husband slumped in his rocker with a glum look on his face.

"Hi, Hetty. Something wrong with Kurt?" Suzanne asked

"Oh, he's still grousing about the robbery."

"You mean the burglary over at Audrey Hing's place?"

"No. Here!" said Hetty. "Someone broke into *our* house and took Kurt's prize 35mm camera. All the lovely photos he took are gone. And as if that wasn't enough, they took his iPad and tablet computer, too."

"Wow! When did this happen?" asked Suzanne.

"Two weeks ago last Tuesday. Kurt has been nuts ever since.

You won't believe how the thief got in. The cops think he shinnied up the drainpipe to our lanai roof and removed the screen to the second-story bathroom. From there he had access to the entire house." She leaned on her broom, bending the nylon bristles.

"Aren't you glad you weren't here when he broke in?" asked Suzanne, then added in an offhand way, "I would assume all that stuff is replaceable."

"Tell that to the brooding zombie over there," muttered Hetty. "It's not just the money. It's all the time he spent shopping for just the right things."

Suzanne nodded absently. "Say, did you hear about the earthquake?" she asked

"Yes. The *Fox News* weatherman mentioned it about half an hour ago. Said there could be a tsunami, but it would take a couple days to get here and there's no telling how big and strong that tidal wave might be."

"Well," Suzanne said, "if it's anything like the one last year, we have nothing to worry about. Remember how everyone panicked and ran to the grocery stores and loaded up on toilet paper and rice?" She laughed. "The storm never reached us. Next day everyone went back to the markets and tried to return all the stuff."

Hetty nodded. "The TV announcers made a big deal about a little stream overflowing in Hilo. We stayed up 'til 3 a.m. waiting for something big to happen and all we ever saw was the two reporters sitting at their desks. It was stupid."

"You're so right," Suzanne said. "See ya." She took off once more and covered nearly a mile before a late-model sedan slowed and stopped next to her on the access road.

Naomi Waihea rolled down the passenger-side window. "Say, Suzanne, I'm in a serious pickle. We need a babysitter for Kimo this coming Thursday evening and we've tried every teenager within five miles. I know you don't make a practice of it, but it would only be for three hours."

"Isn't he old enough to stay home by himself now?"

"After the Miller place next door got burglarized, we're afraid to leave him home alone."

"We'd pay you, too," said her husband, leaning in her direction from behind the wheel.

"Sorry," Suzanne said. She hated babysitting, and didn't much care for their kid either. "I might have to work that night shift. We're short-handed. Maybe next time, Naomi."

The car drove off, and Suzanne pressed on.

When she neared the Hing house, she decided she would turn back; a four-mile run was enough for today. She'd work with her hand weights and resistance band later this evening. As the handsome stucco dwelling on half an acre came into view, she saw a police cruiser and crime scene truck parked in the circular driveway. Audrey Hing and her teenage son, Stanley, were batting a volleyball back and forth over a net at the side of the house. As Suzanne started her turn toward home, she heard Audrey call out, "Wait!"

Tossing the ball to her son, she hastened toward Suzanne. "Did you hear what happened to us last night? Someone broke into the house and stole my best jewelry. Heirlooms I inherited from my mother. Other things, too."

Stanley, in T-shirt and cut-off shorts, tucked the ball under one arm and joined his mother. "My laptop, my camera, and the Rolex Dad gave me for my birthday. A real bummer."

Recently widowed, Audrey looked despondent. "If only my Jon was still here. We were thinking of putting in an alarm system, but hadn't gotten around to it yet." She brushed a stray strand of hair from her worried face. "We were out, thank goodness. Otherwise we could have been murdered!"

"Yes. The whole neighborhood seems to know about it," Suzanne said. "But I think the robber was more interested in loot than in threatening your lives."

Audrey shot her a quizzical look. "How would you know that?"

Suzanne shrugged. "Just a guess. I assume you're adequately insured."

"Of course. But still, I feel personally violated." Audrey swept a manicured hand over her tailored slacks and silk shirt. "Isn't it ridiculous? I'm out here playing volleyball like this because the police wanted us out of the house and out of the way while they were dusting for prints and whatever else they do."

"How did they get in, the thieves, I mean?"

"Suzanne, I'm ashamed to tell you. It was all my fault. When I went out to my bridge club, I backed the car out of the garage and forgot to use the remote to close it. And on top of that, I didn't lock the door inside the garage that leads to our back hall. Whoever did this just walked in. So careless of me."

Not knowing quite how to respond and eager to get away, Suzanne changed the subject. "Did you know they're predicting a tsunami watch for late tomorrow or the next day? Take care you two." She waved, wheeled about, and returned to the running path.

Her long legs and lanky body easily conquered the final two miles home as she visualized a glass of white Zinfandel, then a heat-and-eat Salisbury steak supper. The way back proved uneventful; the sun, glowing red, was falling into the distant ocean, and the rest of the neighbors had disappeared into their homes.

The next morning, Suzanne arrived at work to find a "See me" note signed with a sprawling "B" propped on her computer keyboard. She stepped cautiously into Bart's office, expecting to be chewed out for something. Instead, he greeted her pleasantly.

"Sit down, Suzanne." Perched on a corner of his desk, he said, "I just got wind of a big protest group convening on Maui, in Lahaina. They're against all the new high-rise construction. Saying it'll ruin the character of the island. I want you to cover the story. Take a few days, get good quotes."

Suzanne tried to object. "There's a huge storm coming. You know, from the earthquake in Japan."

A foul expression crossed Bart's clean-shaven face, a clear sign that the assignment was not negotiable. "It's all speculation. We might not get any of it."

Suzanne caught a late inter-island flight to Maui.

Two days later, at 8:30 in the morning, the storm hit the Hawaiian islands. Kaua'i first, then O'ahu. Winds of 135 miles an hour, followed by what was most feared: a treacherous tsunami. The monster waves damaged many vulnerable homes along the Sunset Beach shoreline, but none so badly as Suzanne's cottage, sitting closest to the water's edge. It bore the brunt of both the wind and the twenty-foot wave that followed. Early on, its ramshackle lanai crumbled into so much driftwood and soon disappeared altogether. The mighty wave broke out the glass in every window, allowing it to freely wash through the bungalow, driving most of the furniture against the front wall. Coarse sand slipped away from one of the main pilings supporting the oceanside corner of the house until the entire post became nakedly exposed. It shamefully collapsed, dropping first that portion of the floor, then a chunk of roof above it.

Inside, the water-logged bedroom ceiling collapsed, carrying with it a huge steamer trunk that had been stored in the crawl space under the roof. The brute force of the trunk landing on the floor cracked it open in several places like a dropped raw egg.

Fifteen minutes later, the ocean ebbed itself free of O'ahu's North Shore, leaving behind wreckage, rubble, and gaping holes where young trees had stood.

* * * *

Around noon, the sun and a few optimistic, puffy clouds returned to the skies. A group of curious, concerned neighbors trudged along Kam Highway. They halted, stunned, opposite Suzanne's ravaged bungalow. Cautiously, the group sloshed through ankle-deep water to the small front lawn and peered inside the gaping, empty picture window.

Mr. Makamura hastily joined them from next door; his own sturdy house had survived intact. He was the first to speak. "Poor Missy Lumi. She not deserve dis. She good people, good neighbor."

"I agree," said Bjorn Pettersen, the tow-headed surfer. "I wonder where Suzy is. I haven't seen her for a couple days."

"She's on Maui," said Hetty Burger. "She told me that new boss of hers likes sending her off-island for feature stories. It's going to be some kind of shock coming home to this."

"Yah," said her husband, Kurt.

"Maybe we should try to help her clean up some of the mess before she comes home," said Grace Kalaheo.

"That's a great idea," said Naomi Waihea, taking the first steps toward the front door.

"Wait!" shouted Micah, Naomi's husband. "This is crazy. We don't know how safe the joint is. It could collapse while we're in there. That stanchion on the left has already caved. We could get hurt."

"He's right, you know," added Audrey Hing. "We shouldn't be so quick to risk our necks."

"Aw, come on, Mom," Stanley, said. "Don't be such a sissy."

Audrey glared. "Young man, I'll thank you to show me some respect."

"I know Suzy will appreciate it," Hetty said. "We just have to be careful."

Bjorn tried the door. Ironically, it was still locked.

"I guess we can't get in," Naomi said, looking rather pleased that they were off the hook.

"No problem!" Stanley said. Without waiting for permission from his mother, the youth nimbly climbed through the large picture window, narrowly avoiding the remaining shards of glass still stuck in the frame. Once inside, he set about clearing away the furniture blocking the front door: a crushed end table, mangled floor lamp, and a sopping-wet easy chair. He unlocked the deadbolt, the locked button in the knob, and opened the door.

Outside, Micah adjusted the peaked cap on his thick gray hair. He didn't move. Squinting behind wire-rimmed glasses, he said, "Hold on a minute, folks. This could be construed as breaking-and-entering."

"Oh, Micah," his wife snapped, "don't nitpick. We're just trying to help Suzanne out."

"Besides," Mr. Makamura added, "there was no breaking. Only entering. The window already broken."

Micah knew he'd been outnumbered. One by one, the group of nine slowly fed through the fresh access and shuffled about as best they could to assess the inside damage. Their sandals squished against the thoroughly soaked floor. They avoided the kitchenette; all the cupboard doors had sprung open. Littering the tiny floor space were pots, pans, broken dishes, soup cans, and drenched boxes of cereal. In the living room Grace picked up a dustpan. Hetty grabbed a flat plywood board. Together they tried to shovel some of the mounds of sand out through the rear windows, naked without their panes. A futile attempt, given the weight of the wet sand and their primitive tools.

Grace, a tall woman with a single braid down her back, got to the bedroom first. She saw the twin bed skewed on its side against the back wall. Then she shouted: "Hey, guys! Look! There's a huge steamer trunk in here. It must have fallen through that big hole in the ceiling up there. How about a couple of you young muscle-men coming in here to move it?"

Kurt and Bjorn positioned themselves at opposite ends of the trunk, gripping the leather handles. "Ready?" asked Bjorn. "Ready," Kurt replied. But they had only hefted the trunk a few inches when the crack that had developed on impact with the floor suddenly split wide. The bottom burst open and the contents spewed out.

Grace was standing in a corner, watching. "Guys!" she screamed. "What is all this? It's full of jewelry. Lots of it. It looks like the real thing, expensive stuff, I'll bet." Her scream brought the rest of the group squeezing into the room. The two men dragged the split-apart trunk the few feet to the side wall. A trail of the contents kept spewing out, like a lava flow from a crater.

Now all nine neighbors were crouching, kneeling, squatting, not caring how sandy, muddy, and wet their clothes got. Hetty gasped, bent over, and picked up a gold charm bracelet. After examining it closely, she turned to her husband. "Kurt? Isn't this just like the bracelet you gave me last Valentine's Day?"

Kurt's brushy black mustache twitched. "Look for an inscription on the charm and you'll know if it's yours," he said.

Hetty's eyes watered as she read aloud. "You're still gorgeous, your loving Kurt."

Naomi's heart skipped a beat as she picked up a blue star-sapphire ring. "This is mine. I didn't even know we were robbed. I thought I'd misplaced it. My grandparents gave it to me for my high school graduation."

"Well, I'll be damned," Micah said. "It looks like this is all stolen jewelry."

"What the devil is Suzy doing with this stuff?" asked Bjorn.

"Der mus' be some explaining," Mr. Makamura said. "Missy no thief."

Audrey dove into the pile with two hands. "Oh my God!" she whispered, pulling out a large black velvet pouch. Untying the silk strings, she peered inside. "My diamond and ruby broach. My pearl necklace. My diamond tiara that I wore to the opera ball. And the cocktail ring Jon gave me for our twentieth anniversary." She began to sob.

Naomi pressed forward. "I don't believe this. My turquoise pendant, and one of the matching earrings. Micah! Help me find the other one."

On his knees, her husband sifted through dozens of pieces, but found only his college class ring.

Bjorn surveyed the lot and declared, "There's much more here than all of us can possibly claim to own. We'll have to notify the police. Maybe we shouldn't remove any of the jewels—they're evidence."

Abruptly, Micah stood up, hands on hips, his faded jeans caked with wet sand. "He's right. We need to stop. If it's all stolen, we're messing around with evidence, disturbing a crime scene."

"You're not a criminal lawyer, are you, Micah?" Grace asked.

"No, Grace, I'm a family practice attorney, but I do know a little something about criminal law." His voice came out more biting than he'd intended.

Grace's narrow face flushed; she wasn't used to being scolded. "Thieves got into my house last month. But I haven't found anything of mine yet."

Audrey put her arm around her friend's shoulders. "We'll

help you. Let's just wait for the police."

"I'll call it in," Bjorn said. "I've got my cell phone." He stumbled out to the living room.

"What's still in the trunk?" persisted Grace. She was a teacher, fortyish, living paycheck to paycheck.

Kurt turned one broken section of the trunk on end and wrestled both buckle clamps open. Inside, they found a number of large drawers still intact. Grace pulled one open, and Stanley, looking over her shoulder, shouted, "There's my laptop!"

"My new iPad!" Grace blurted out. "And my portable DVD player. Thank heaven!"

In a second drawer they discovered several tablet computers, three of the latest iPhones in glitzy covers, and two miniature cameras. A third drawer yielded a small presentation projector, the latest version. Drawers four through seven held yet more jewelry.

A distraught Mr. Makamura shuffled out, his shoulders hunched. He shook his head in disbelief. "There must be some explaining. Missy, she good lady."

Bjorn finished his call to the police, and was told they were on their way.

"Good job, Bjorn," nodded Micah. "Let's all go outside. We need to greet the police and explain everything. We don't want anyone else second-guessing us. We're witnesses."

Unheard and unseen by the neighbors milling around the meager lawn, a canary-colored Mini crept down the street. It crunched over and around the debris, stopping at the curb fifty feet away, unable to get any closer. The driver's door didn't open for several minutes as the occupant observed the devastation that lay before her. Then Suzanne emerged. Her bungalow! She hardly recognized it. The front stanchion on the left had buckled, as if the structure were resting on one praying knee. Where was her lanai? So horrified, she didn't notice the two police cruisers pulling up behind her Mini.

Suzanne became the target of nine pairs of eyes, their accusing stares. These were her neighbors, her friends, especially Mr. Makamura. Why were they staring at her?

But she knew why, of course. *Oh for God's sake. Why did I keep the stuff so long? Why didn't I fence it all right away? There goes my job. Maybe even my nice life here. Would they believe I was just holding the trunk for a friend? That I had no idea what was inside? But what friend? And how stupid would I be not to have looked inside? Well, folks, this is not over yet. It's not like I've been hiding a body or anything.*

As she approached, Suzanne Lumi took a deep breath to compose herself. She arranged her features into a sweet, innocent, wide-eyed look, and in a soft, childlike voice, asked, "What?"

"Who the hell do you think you're kidding?" shouted Grace as the officers led Suzanne away.

"Maybe Missy not so good lady," said Mr. Makamura with tears running down his cheeks.

Roses

Morgan Peetry didn't enjoy jogging. He was only doing it to forget. His girlfriend had just dumped him most cruelly. Louise had the looks of a Grecian goddess and the tightest *tush*, the most tantalizing breasts of anyone he'd ever dated. She possessed all the qualities he wanted in a woman. Except one: her constant nagging to change him into someone he wasn't.

"Morgan, your love handles have turned into spare tires. I'm outta here." His flabby waist was the last straw for her.

Morgan blubbered his rejection to his best friend, who said, "Go on a diet. And jog—at Magic Island. You'll love it."

Morgan decided dieting wouldn't be too hard. He wasn't dating anyone and going out to restaurants. Up to now his idea of jogging had been from his living room couch to the fridge. Slowly pulling on shorts, T-shirt, and a University of Hawaii Warriors cap, he sighed. *Maybe it'll take my mind off Louise.*

Magic Island is a small peninsula jutting out from Ala Moana beach park that sprawls between downtown Honolulu and Waikiki. The jogging/walking path approximates three-quarters of a mile. Two laps, a mile and a half, are just right for beginners. Supposedly. On his first day out, Morgan trudged along the Ala Wai Canal side, not even aware of the stunning views of Diamond Head and the Pacific Ocean.

He had to face the fact that he was inherently uncoordinated and had too little endurance. He made a clumsy attempt at a lope, but it evolved into an uneven sole-scraping trot. Even the trot lasted only half a minute. He had to replace it with a *shlepping* walk. Determined not to quit, he pushed himself along the path beside the lagoon, not even noticing the locals barbequing under umbrella-shaped monkeypod trees and the air wafting the scent of teriyaki sauce.

On his snail-paced second lap around, an overheated Morgan dragged himself up the asphalt path to the seawall. A few feet away, he spotted a freshly painted green steel bench with its inviting back and armrests. An anxious debate roiled in his mind—whether to stop and rest or to trudge on and finish the last third of a mile. The nearer he came to the bench, the more tempting it looked. A no-brainer! Eyes half-closed from the blazing sun, sticky sweat gluing his T-shirt to his chest, he flopped down on the bench, oblivious of his surroundings. His expectations seemed so unattainable and his progress so immeasurable. It was all one big downer.

Succumbing to exhaustion, Morgan relaxed there for a while and might have even dozed off, except that, in the next moment, a great wave happened to crash among the lava boulders below, sending a spritz of sea water over the top of the seawall and across his face and bare limbs. He wiped away the annoying salty spray with the back of his hand. But the spray had brought with it a refreshing rinse and, gradually, he began to feel better about himself and his prospects. He glanced about and took in his surroundings for the first time.

Straight ahead an ocean tug hauled a heavily loaded container barge into Honolulu harbor. A suspended parasailer moved gracefully below the clouds. A surfer opted for an ideal wave to ride. And at the opposite end of the bench where he sat there lay a single long-stemmed rosebud. *How come I didn't notice it when I first sat down?* Obviously, it had not been in the sun long; it had not begun to wilt.

Morgan began to obsess and fantasize about the lone rose. Was it a sign of a dawning romance? Then why had it been forgotten?

Or was it the opposite—a young woman renouncing her engagement? Worse yet, was it an omen, plunging him into a life devoid of anyone capable of loving him? Just then the prevailing wind, mixed with ocean spray, shifted in a single gust toward the lonely young man, sending a shuddering chill through him. Standing up to shake off the dampness, he nearly ran into another jogger. The full-figured young woman adjusted her course and continued on past him without acknowledging his existence. At first he felt slighted. *What am I, invisible?* Then he realized he was being paranoid and decided to continue his own jogging. But his eyes drifted to the lone rose sitting there on the bench. Morgan scooped it up and returned to the running path.

By now the woman had a considerable head start on him. But as he trotted, his pace picked up, and he began to close the space between them. Morgan had actually begun to jog and almost run. He couldn't be sure why. He fixated on the ponytail, swinging from side to side like a pendulum, and then on her *tush*, hypnotically gyrating one way and reversing with each pair of steps. Her chunky thighs and rounded calves appealed to him as he drew even closer. Soon he fell into step about ten feet behind her and trailed her for about fifty yards.

The woman moved to her right, hoping he would pass her. When he didn't, she kept turning her head to see if he was still behind her. At first, fear shot through her mind, then anger took hold. She stopped and spun around to face him. With the sudden stop, he very nearly ran her over. Standing face to face, no more than a foot apart, she laced into him. "Why in blazes are you stalking me?" Her cheeks flushed and her blue eyes glared with contempt.

Morgan hastened to explain. "Hey! I wasn't stalking you and I wasn't really aware of following you. I merely tried to match your pace. *Gee, she has a pretty face,* he thought. *Even when she's pissed off.* "I'm still new at this sort of thing," he added.

"What sort of thing?"

"I only meant that I'm new to jogging and I'm experimenting with different pacing. I don't have any hidden agenda and I don't mean you any harm."

"So bug off and stay away from me." Her protest came out a bit weak. *He sounds sincere enough,* she thought. *An educated vocabulary anyway.*

"I apologize," he said. "Here, would this make up for my behavior?" He held the rose out to her. "I found it lying on a bench back there. Maybe you'd like it."

Abruptly, her expression went blank as recalculation clicked through her mind. She acknowledged the young man for the first time and sized him up. *Tall, not bad looking, a bit chubby, but who am I to complain? He could be telling the truth.* She didn't know why, but accepted the rose and stuck the long stem in her fanny pack strap. They began to walk side by side for the last quarter-mile to the parking lot.

"I'm Morgan, Morgan Peetry, if you're the least bit interested in knowing me."

"I'm Nancy Helman. We'll see how it goes from here."

At the parking lot Morgan asked her, "Want to go for coffee?"

"Thanks, but I have to get to work."

"What do you do?" he asked.

"I'm a receptionist for a doctor."

" Will you be here tomorrow at the same time?"

"I plan to be."

"Me too."

She held out her hand for him to shake.

He took it. They cautiously shook clammy hands and parted for their respective cars.

* * * *

The next morning Morgan showered and shaved extra close, slapping on his best aftershave, and carefully combing his thick brown hair. He skipped breakfast in the remote hope that Nancy would join him for it later. On his way to the park he stopped at a lei shop for a single American Beauty rose. He arrived at the park early and chose a bench near the start of the path so he could watch for her arrival.

The time came and the time went without Nancy. He waited an extra hour to be sure before starting to trot up the path. His logy pace and frequent walking stretches reflected his mood. *Nancy ditched me. She wasn't interested in me at all.* By the time he completed the first lap, Morgan was finished for the day. But he didn't want to give up on Nancy, so when he reached his car, he sat there making up excuses for her. *Maybe she's sick, or she had an important errand to take care of, or her boss wanted her to come in early.*

The next day Morgan repeated his routine with the purchase of a single red rose and was again disappointed. As he passed the bench where he first saw her he turned back and laid the rose there. He repeated the same scenario for the next two days. Nancy didn't show up and that made him angry. *What am I, chopped liver?* Each day he took to the path anyway, and a strange thing happened. The angrier he got, the faster he jogged, until his clumsy half-trotting eventually disappeared and became a strong, rhythmic pace.

On the fifth day Morgan didn't bother with the rose, but came to the park anyway. He had almost completed the first lap along the Ala Wai Canal when he saw her—waiting at the start of the path along the lagoon. Without a word, she fell in beside him and matched his pace. They jogged silently, side by side, until they reached the bench with the four roses, now quite wilted. As they approached it, Morgan scooped them up, wrapped the stems in a clean handkerchief, and presented them to Nancy.

She accepted the drooping roses, jogged a few feet more, and then came to a complete halt. Morgan stopped a few feet farther and turned to face her. She closed the space between them, leaned forward, and kissed him on the cheek. "You're very sweet," she murmured.

His fingers touched his cheek, as if to feel her kiss, but he was still ticked off. "How can you say that when you stood me up for four days?"

She skirted the question. "Did you know that Nancy is married?"

"Hell, no!" *Why is she speaking to me in the third person?*

"Hey, what's going on here?"

"Did you know that I'm not her?"

"What're you talking about? You are Nancy, aren't you?"

"No. I'm her twin sister."

"No way! Identical!"

"Yeah."

"Wow!" exclaimed Morgan. His eyes flicked over her. *Same fair skin with freckles sprinkled on her cheeks. Same auburn ponytail. Same appealing zaftig figure.* But he still felt suspicious. "So why did your sister show an interest in me?"

The young woman shrugged. "Afterward she felt stupid. She'd had an argument with her husband that morning. She told me about you, Morgan. You made quite an impression on her. She liked you and thought we might hit it off."

Morgan frowned. "I assumed she changed her mind and just decided to forget the whole thing. But why did you wait so many days to come here?"

"I couldn't make it before now and I had no way of getting in touch with you."

"Well, if you're not Nancy, what *is* your name?"

"Francine Helman, but I go by Francy and I am single."

Wow! Nancy and Francy. "Do you want to go for coffee now, Francy?"

She flipped her ponytail forward and shyly said, "I'd rather go out this evening if it's okay with you."

"You mean a real date? A movie and supper?"

"Yeah!"

He grinned. Suddenly, the day looked rosy.

Temptation

Freemont Rankin III, a well-known Midwest philanthropist, went to his grave looking and feeling as fit as a thirty-five-year-old. No one protested that his demise wasn't natural. Why would anyone protest? Even if they had, the police would have just laughed. Freemont lived to be ninety-six and had passed to another world peacefully while sleeping in his own bed. There was no evidence to suggest foul play. No one came forward to challenge the doctor's findings of heart failure. A negative preliminary toxicology screen satisfied the medical examiner as well.

But family and friends harbored a secret fear about Freemont, an eerie, unexplained phenomenon. For nearly ten years before he died, he continually predicted the exact date, place, and hour of his death. Whenever anyone confronted him about his prediction, Freemont simply laughed and said, "That's when my contract will be up." And so it was.

Four days after his funeral and burial, immediate family members received an official invitation. "You are invited to the offices of Morton, Bagley, and Shultz, Attorneys at Law, to hear the reading of Freemont Rankin III's Last Will and Testament.

A week later, on the specified day, they gathered in the firm's office, where attorney Walter Bagley read the contents to the apparent heirs. Essentially, Freemont's last will divided his wealth in the following manner. The grand mansion and two luxury cars went to his young trophy wife. His beach house, a car, and a sailboat went to his ditsy debutante daughter. The mountain cabin, a power boat, and a motorcycle went to his alcoholic son. Five charities received generous bequests, and so did a number of loyal servants and employees. The attorney announced all these bequests without ever mentioning the name of Philip Rankin, his nephew.

Philip had no idea why he had been invited to this august gathering. The Rankin brothers—his father and Freemont—had never gotten along, and as a result, the two families had minimal, always frosty, contact. Also, there was the great financial divide. Philip's father, Escher, modestly provided for his wife and son, but he and Freemont lived in different worlds. Escher and his wife budgeted, scrimped, and scraped by. Years earlier, Escher had borrowed a large sum of money at a mercilessly high interest rate from Freemont, but couldn't pay it back. Freemont never forgave him.

Philip struggled financially through a state college and graduate school. He had spent his past four summers interning with various corporations and recently received his MBA. Unfortunately, his education had left him with a mountain of debt in student loans.

Nevertheless, his parents crowed with delight at his accomplishments and God-given gifts. At age twenty-four, their son had smarts and good looks. Tall and lean, he had blue eyes and brown hair that fluffed up slightly with a mind of its own. Wire-rimmed glasses gave him an earnest, trustworthy look.

Philip sat quietly through the reading of his uncle's will, thinking he was the forgotten relative, one more embarrassment staged against his family. Then he heard his name. Everyone looked around the room searching for him, for no one recognized his face after so many years of his family's exile. He raised his hand, and a secretary asked to see his driver's license. Satisfied, she handed him an envelope with his name typed across the front. He slit the edge of the envelope open with his pocket penknife and removed a note folded over a second envelope. The note, typed on the law firm's letterhead stationery, wasted no space on pleasantries.

"You are to follow these instructions precisely and immediately. Go to 2314 Eden Place and present the sealed inner envelope to the receptionist in the lobby."

Philip frowned. This abrupt, strange command deserved an explanation. He waited until all the heirs had left the office and approached Walter Bagley for clarification.

"Young man," Bagley replied, his voice huffy, "I've been Freemont's attorney for more than fifty years, but he never said a word to me about any bequest to you, nor even a hint about the contents of that inner envelope. He told me only that I was to deliver these instructions to you after his death. As for that address, I haven't a clue. I would guess a select few of Freemont's associates might have offices there, but again, I have no idea what purpose they serve. Your uncle's secrets have been literally locked in stone for years. Even my partners in this firm are completely in the dark. Sorry." With a shrug of his shoulders Bagley walked away.

Three hours later Philip Rankin stood in front of 2314 Eden Place. Trying not to look anxious, and determined to act businesslike, he was still dressed in his navy-blue suit with white shirt and subdued tie. He crossed the street to get a better look at this mysterious edifice before entering. The granite and concrete building, a somber gray, stood at least twenty-five stories high amid the commercial, governmental, and residential high-rises congregated in the city's center. A broad ring of black marble banded its midsection halfway up. An imposing bronze tetrahedron—a pyramid with four sides—capped off the very top.

Who are the select few Mr. Bagley talked about? Philip wondered. *What are they hiding? And why?* Still clutching the note in one hand, Philip crossed the street and pushed through the revolving door into the high-ceilinged lobby. He scanned the building's directory, searching intently for a familiar name. He found none among the first five floors of commercial enterprises, nor any in the remaining residential suites above that floor. At the desk in the lobby, he handed the unopened envelope to the receptionist, who looked like a

Barbie Doll come to life. She smiled mechanically as she opened the envelope and read the note inside.

"Oh, yes. We've been expecting you, Mr. Rankin." With a gold ballpoint pen, she wrote several lines on a piece of paper, folded it over once, and handed it to him, along with the original envelope. "Wait until you are alone—when there's no one else waitng on the ground floor," she said, "and take the elevator on your left. Further instructions are contained in my note. Thank you for your patience."

Philip pushed the call button for his elevator, and decided he'd better read the instructions the receptionist had just written for him. "Insert the key in the elevator's control panel and turn it to the OFF position...." The elevator on the left arrived, and the door slid open to an empty car before he could read more. *What key?* With trembling hands, he searched the envelope and found that a cylindrical key had been slipped inside by the receptionist. Philip used it to turn off the elevator's power. Luckily, that maneuver did not douse the recessed ceiling light, for he had more to read: "Now proceed to the thirteenth floor."

One glance at the control panel told him there *was* no thirteenth floor. The display went from twelve to fourteen, and then contiguously on to twenty-six. His stomach began to churn, but he dared not stop now. He read on. "Depressing the fifth and eighth floor buttons simultaneously will grant you access to the thirteenth floor. When you are through reading, you may turn the power back on, remove the key, and proceed with the remainder of your instructions. Please return the key to the receptionist in the lobby when you leave the building."

Philip pressed buttons five and eight together, and the elevator started up. He watched as the control panel flashed indicator lights for lobby through ten, then eleven and twelve. The elevator stopped—surprisingly, with no panel light at all. The door slid back to reveal a massive curved desk with a corporate name high on the wall behind it: "Other-World Accommodations, Ltd." Under the corporate name, a sculpture of two golden wings enveloped a fiery urn—filled with live, flickering flames. Below it, in bronze letters:

"**Dr. Be'el Zee Hades, Chief Operating Officer.**"

A young woman with lush auburn locks rose from her chair to reveal a voluptuous body in a clinging silver lamé gown. Unlike any secretary Philip had ever known.

"Ah, Mr. Rankin," she said. "I'm Jezebel. You may call me Jez. We've been expecting you. Dr. Zee is anxious to meet you. Follow me, and I'll take you to him."

Philip felt as though he were walking through a cloud—in some other world, like the sign said. Glancing through open doors, he saw only empty rooms. All the furniture and walls were painted off-white, favoring a pinkish tinge. Oddly, he saw neither a window nor a light fixture, yet the lighting seemed naturally bright.

Jez led him down a long hall, its walls hung with gilt-framed portraits of somber-looking men and women. At one point, Philip could have sworn he recognized Freemont Rankin's face in one of them. He couldn't rightly be sure as his eyes were hypnotically drawn to Jez's coquettish swaying hips as he followed her. They passed through an enormous work area with dozens of employees of both genders milling about, all clad in white. Philip's breath caught in his chest. Every last one of the workers was uniquely stunning in his or her own right. At last, Jez stopped in front of a closed door. As she raised her hand to knock, the door opened without her slightest touch. Yet no one was standing on the other side to have opened it.

As they stepped inside, Philip saw a strikingly handsome man with black hair, sharp features, and a black goatee. He looked to be about forty and was seated behind a gleaming mahogany desk with no papers or anything else that looked like work on it. Philip saw only a computer monitor and keyboard.

"Thank you, Jez, that will be all," he said. Then his gaze turned from the large monitor to engage his visitor.

Philip felt a sudden chill. The man had emerald-green, glowing eyes.

"Welcome, Philip. Have a seat." He pointed to a leather armchair in front of his desk. "I am known as Dr. Zee."

"That's nice, but why am I here?" Philip asked.

"You were curious, I assume. You came here of your own free will, didn't you?"

"Yes, but I was instructed to." Philip began to fidget.

"You didn't have to follow those instructions, did you, my boy? Ergo, you came of your own free will."

"I suppose you're right. I'm anxious to find out what Uncle Freemont left me."

Dr. Zee's radiating eyes abruptly captured Philip's attention and held them prisoner. He sneered. "Your uncle left you absolutely nothing. He merely recommended you to me. I, on the other hand, can be of great service and benefit to you, Philip."

"How's that? What do you mean, Dr. Zee?"

"Did you ever notice that your uncle possessed four of life's most sought-after desires?"

"I don't understand. I didn't know him all that well. Our families didn't get along."

"Your uncle had health, wealth, good looks, and everlasting sexual prowess. Especially, the ways he pleased his thirty-five-year-old wife and kept her in extravagant style. Don't you agree?"

Philip frowned. "That much everyone knew about him, by reputation. But what's that got to do with anything? Wait! Dr. Zee, are you claiming you had something to do with all that?"

"Now, my boy, you're beginning to see the bigger picture." He stroked his perfectly groomed goatee.

Philip squinted skeptically. "What did all that wealth, power, and extra prowess cost Uncle Freemont? What did *you* get out of it? And by the way, I'm assuming you're not a medical doctor."

Dr. Zee's thin lips turned up at the corners, but his expression remained hard. "You assume correctly. Getting back to your uncle, let's just say he was—no, still is, my protégé. He was extremely useful to me in your world and remains so in mine. Of course, in another form and way now."

"Useful how?"

"Now, now, my boy, propriety prevents me from going into the nitty-gritty specifics. I'll tell you what. I'll bring up his contract."

Dr. Zee's manicured fingers diddled a number of taps on a keyboard. He turned to observe the monitor on his left. "Ah, here it is. Freemont contracted for a maximum of ten evils. Ten times during his extended lifetime I asked him to commit ten deliciously evil acts, and he willingly complied. Of course, he could have contracted for fewer evils for proportionately fewer years of lavish living."

Philip could feel cold drops of sweat forming in his armpits under his clean shirt. "If you claim he still is your protégé, where is my uncle now?"

"At the moment I have him out on assignment. He won't be back until Thursday."

Philip's voice took on a frantic tone. "Dr. Zee, this is insane. What are you talking about? My uncle is dead."

Dr. Zee's eyes glittered. "Only in a manner of speaking, dear boy. Special circumstances are involved."

Philip rose a few inches out of the chair. "What special circumstances? And why would my deceased uncle recommend *me* to *you?*"

"Most probably, it had nothing to do with you personally. More likely, he was squeezing out a little more hatred of your father. One last dig at his brother, so to speak. That's one of the things I like most about your uncle."

"But what could you possibly want from me?"

"Well, you do have many of Freemont's genes. You needn't stay poor all your life. Besides, I'm an equal opportunity employer. I do unto everyone equally and without bias."

Philip couldn't tell whether Dr. Zee was smiling or sneering. The slur against his honest, hard-working dad offended him. "Who says I'll always be poor? I have my MBA and I have some pretty good management skills. But I assume you know that. Am I correct that you'll want me to sign something—in blood, too?" he added in a mocking voice, expecting Dr. Zee to join him in the joke.

Dr. Zee didn't. "Yes, of course. He pulled open a drawer, extracted a sheaf of forms, along with a syringe, and laid them on the desk. "I happen to have a contract right here, fresh from our legal section. You won't mind the syringe. I don't like using ink. It's so unreliable."

"Wait!" Philip burst in. "There's something I've never understood. What business was Uncle Freemont in? How did he make his millions?"

Dr. Zee's crystalline eyes projected a stinging intensity. "Your uncle was a slumlord, Philip. He specialized in evicting poor people from their apartments. Then he tore down the decrepit buildings and sold the valuable land to developers for luxury high-rises and extracted a generous prize for his efforts."

Philip cocked his head in confusion. "But what if some tenants protested? What if they had legitimate leases and refused to move?"

Dr. Zee placed his long fingers in the prayer position. "Oh, I made a provision for difficult tenants, and your uncle carried out my instructions impeccably. Those tenants met up with unforeseeable lethal accidents, especially those who were living in fifth- or sixth-floor walkups—unfortunate cases of falling out a window or down a steep stairwell. One ground-floor tenant even fell in front of a fast-moving bus. Each one appeared as a terrible mishap, of course. Such a shame. Your uncle had the expertise at all levels to clear a building—and he continues that business for me now. And so can you, my boy. Now, let's get started on your contract."

"That's not exactly the kind of life I had in mind for myself. Don't you have any less drastic a position for me?" Philip asked, his voice twisted with irony. He didn't expect the serious response.

Dr. Zee raised his pointed black eyebrows. "Son, I'll tell you what I'm going to do. I'll erase one evil for every five you sign up for. I'll make you rich. Don't you think that's fair?"

Philip began to feel the pressure. *The man's creepy. I've got to stall him and get out of here.* He murmured, "I'd like to sleep on anything this important before I sign up."

"That's not possible," snapped Dr. Zee. "I can't let you leave without signing. Decline and once you leave the building, you will lose all memory of me and ever having been here."

Philip finally understood why he'd been invited to the reading of the will. He'd been singled out and invited here to tempt him into following in his uncle's footsteps. He glared at Dr. Zee. "And what happens to those who dare resist? Is this an invitation to be murdered?" He crossed his arms over his chest and lowered his head. "Do what you will to me, Dr. Zee. I'm not signing anything."

Dr. Zee sprang up, towering, menacing. "As much as I'd like to, I can't force you. I can't detain you. You came here of your own free will, and I have to let you leave of your own free will. I have no power over you unless you do sign."

"In that case I'll leave now," said Philip.

Philip stood, turned away and strode back to the elevator without seeing another soul, living or otherwise. Even the gorgeous Jez had disappeared. He rode down to the lobby, dropped off the key at the desk as instructed, and spun through the revolving door to the street. Turning to face the building one last time, he tried to remember how he got here and who or what he'd seen inside. He simply couldn't.

As he stood, perplexed, at the curb, Philip's bizarre memories deserted him. The last thing he recalled was sitting through the entire reading of his uncle's will with everyone else in the family receiving bequests. He didn't recall getting anything, or did he? Just then, an exhilarating feeling rippled through him, the kind of fresh lift you get when you've conquered one of your main fears and stood your ground. It lasted while Philip walked away from the building with his long, loping stride. *I'm going to make my own fortune,* he said to himself. *I've got the smarts, degrees, and determination to go places. I don't need anything else from the damned Rankin family.*

Several months later, Philip came across an item in the local paper's business pages. The office building at 2314 Eden Place had been torn down—demolished overnight, and would be replaced by a high-rise apartment house with forgiving, affordable rents.

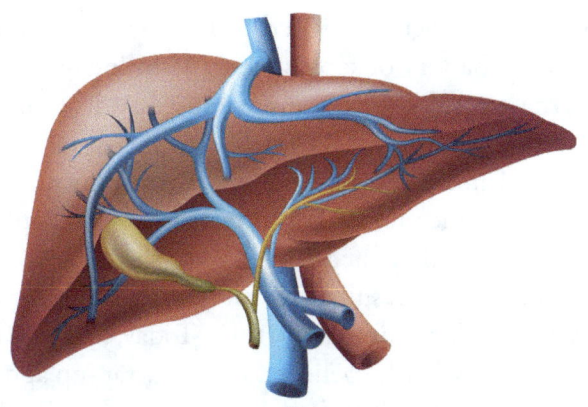

Deliver a Liver

Orville Conners took pride in being a self-made man. This son of a struggling teacher had made his fortune in the software industry, buying up smaller firms and redirecting their assets and talents toward more glamorous outputs. He invested a considerable share of those assets in a young firm called Power Max and took over as chief executive officer. Power Max produced cutting-edge communications software for civilian spacecrafts.

At age thirty-eight, physically toned, and full of energy, Orville had thick ash-blond hair, wide cheeks, and a strong chin. Always eager to be "with it," he had trendy facial hair: a blond mustache sloping down to a neatly clipped blond beard. When he smiled, which was often, his perpetually jovial look belied his hard-driving business temperament. Most likely, he had trained his demeanor to put both competitors and colleagues at ease during tricky negotiations.

Orville was known in the business world as a financial wonder. He had every reason to believe he could go on for decades, amassing fortunes and living his carefree bachelor lifestyle. The other directors on Power Max's board decided their CEO's life should be insured, with the firm as sole beneficiary. They set Orville's worth at fifty million dollars. Of course, no insurance company would take on such term exposure without a thorough physical examination. Orville complied. A physician assigned to him by the insurance company conducted a battery of sophisticated tests, including CT scans and MRIs. These results were transmitted to another physician, a specialist.

As he finished his heart-healthy breakfast of oatmeal, whole wheat toast, orange juice, and decaf coffee, Orville felt confident that he'd just achieved another success. *After all, there isn't anything the matter with me.* The test results were all that remained, and now he could go back to making his next fortune. Today, he sat in the reception room, awaiting what he believed was his wrap-up appointment. *A quick consultation and I'll be back in my own office.* The impatient entrepreneur crossed and uncrossed his long legs and toyed with his diamond tie clasp. After thumbing through *WebMD Magazine*, he tossed it aside. He had no need for such reading material.

"Mr. Conners!" A polished walnut door swung open and a secretary ushered him into Dr. Abel T. Shine's private office.

The doctor sat behind his desk reading several pages, then ran his fingers through his salt-and-pepper hair. Without looking up, he motioned Orville to a wooden armchair opposite him. Orville sat down and studied the doctor's intense concentration as the man read—a body-language skill he himself practiced in his daily business dealings. The stress lines across the doctor's forehead, his pursed lips, and an occasional ever-so-slight head twist, signaled something of concern in what he was reading.

Finally, Dr. Shine added the sheaf of papers to a small pile in a file folder and removed his wire-rimmed glasses. "Mr. Conners, if it weren't for one major factor, you could live to be a hundred. For the most part you have taken excellent care of yourself. You have a body most men would envy, but somehow you have abused your liver."

"My liver?" gasped Orville. "Abused? How?"

"Are you a heavy drinker?" asked Dr. Shine.

"Absolutely not," he replied with annoyance. "I'm a social drinker. Hardly regular and nothing excessive. Just enough to satisfy a celebratory toast or a business closing."

"I see," said the doctor, not wanting to argue, but determined to find out the truth. "How have you been feeling? That is, have you had any unusual symptoms lately?"

Orville hesitated, but decided this was no time for waffling. "Mostly I've felt fine. But I've lost ten pounds. I admit I haven't had my normal appetite. Food doesn't taste all that good these days. I've had a few bouts on and off of nausea. And I've vomited a few times, but I just assumed it was indigestion." Orville leaned forward, his gaze intent. "What do I have, Doc? How bad is it? What can you do for me?"

"Mr. Connors, I'm an oncologist and transplant surgeon. I'm very sorry to inform you that you have an advanced stage of liver cancer brought on by cirrhosis. It can even occur in nondrinkers. What you call mild disturbances in your health are symptoms of liver cancer, which starts in the bile ducts. It's called hepatocellular carcinoma. Do nothing and you'll be dead in six to eight months. What you really need is a transplant."

"Jeezus, Doc. This is a shocker. But okay, I trust your judgment. If you're sure that's the only answer, schedule me for a transplant as soon as possible."

"I'm afraid you don't understand, Mr. Conners. There's a waiting list for donors, a registry that governs who gets the next available liver. You have to sign up and wait like everyone else. Sometimes it takes years, and you don't have that long. Meanwhile, there are treatments we can prescribe: chemotherapy and radiation. But in a case as advanced as yours there are no guarantees."

An angry shadow crossed Orville's bland face. He pounded his fist on the edge of the mahogany desk. "Doctor, I refuse to waste my time on treatments and promises we both know will lead nowhere. You're right, I don't understand. People with good livers die every day. Why can't I just buy one of those? I'm willing to pay the going price, more if necessary."

Dr. Shine scowled. "First of all, not everyone is willing to be a donor. Second, not everyone is a perfect match. Third, not every donor has a healthy liver. Lastly, none of us knows exactly where or when we're going to die."

Orville half-sprang out of his chair. "But that's a sure path to an early grave. I'm not going there. I'm a wealthy man and I'm only thirty-eight. Surely, one or two million dollars will fetch me a new liver."

"I'm sorry, Mr. Conners. What you're proposing is not only unethical, but illegal. I can't have anything to do with your procuring a new liver. However, my nurse practitioner can help you with the paperwork to get your name on the appropriate registry. Dr. Shine rose and said, "I can furnish all necessary test data when that's requested." Navigating around his desk, he placed a comforting hand in the middle of Orville's back and ushered him into an adjoining office.

Nurse Practitioner Wanda Lupino spun around in her swivel chair to face the two men. A thick braid of light-brown hair settled across the left shoulder of her starched white lab coat. "Hello. How might I help you gentlemen?"

"Hello, Wanda," said Dr. Shine. "This is Mr. Orville Conners. I'd like you to assist him with the necessary paperwork that will put him on the national registry for a new liver." Turning to Orville, he added, "I wish you Godspeed, sir." Dr. Shine did an about-face and left the room.

Nurse Practitioner Wanda moved her plumpish body with mechanical efficiency, hiding the vague disappointment in her chosen career. In her early forties, she had assumed that her professional life would have brought her a rich husband by now, but it had never happened. She motioned for Orville to sit, reached for a file drawer to her left, and pulled out the necessary forms. The two began a lengthy question-and-answer session. She filled out the forms for him, directed him to read each paragraph asserting that he had understood it, and pointed out the lines for his signature. Sucking in her breath, Wanda started to ask him another question, then thought better of it. She was aware of the closeness of this large man who looked so strong and confident. Her next words were hushed to almost a whisper.

"Uh...Mr. Conners, the walls are quite thin here, and I couldn't help overhearing part of your conversation. Did you really mean it when you said you were willing to pay two million dollars for a new liver? Or were you just boasting of your wealth?"

Orville shot her a startled look. "Of course, I meant it, but how is that any of your business? Besides, I don't have to boast, young lady. Fortunately, I have the assets to back up that statement."

Wanda's eyes, the color of smoke, shifted away for a second. Calling her "young lady" was truly patronizing. "You're right, Mr. Conners, it is none of my business, but...suppose I could find a way around the national registry. Would you be interested?"

Orville's jaw dropped. "Are you implying there's a black market for livers?"

"Not exactly. But if there were some way a healthy liver could be intercepted, would you agree to a transplant at the aforementioned price?"

Orville studied the nurse's hard-to-read face, wondering if she was casting him into a net of entrapment. "Is your office bugged?"

"Of course not," she snapped, then caught herself and softened her voice. "I'm just trying to help you, Mr. Conners. I'm aware that your case is terminal."

His tense, muscled body settled back into the chair. "I believe we could come to some mutual terms here," he said cautiously. "However, there still is the matter of finding a doctor willing to perform an illegal transplant. That is, someone with more than ample expertise, experience, and access to a fully acceptable medical facility. I couldn't agree to just any hack or a substandard operating room. I wouldn't want anyone taking advantage of my generosity either. And I'm guessing Dr. Shine won't have any knowledge of your proposal."

"No way!" Wanda replied. "He'd fire me on the spot. Maybe even call the police. Mr. Conners, let's just say that all of this conversation is still in its exploratory stage. If it were to become more than that, how would I get in touch with you?"

"My card, Ms. Lupino," offered Orville, as he handed her the embossed contact information.

* * * *

Wanda stepped into her modest four-room apartment, shut

the door behind her, and called out the name of her live-in boyfriend. "Rudy? Rudy?"

"In here, doll," said a voice coming from the bedroom.

"We need to talk," Wanda said, as she closed the distance between them, and tossed her frayed leather purse on the bureau.

The tall, skinny Rudy was applying aftershave to his hollow cheeks as she entered the bedroom. "I'm getting dressed. I've gotta get to work."

Wanda sat down on the bed. "Rudy, you're forty-two. Maybe you won't have to be a low-paid hospital orderly your whole life."

"What are you talking about?"

"Well," she said, "do you love me enough to take a great big risk for me?"

"You know I love you, baby, but what kind of a risk are you talking about?"

"Something that could bring us big bucks."

"How big?"

"One, two million, maybe."

"Yeah, sure," he sneered. "When pigs fly."

"Rudy, do you still have access to the pathology lab where they send all those diseased organs like the livers and kidneys to be analyzed?"

"Yeah. Why do you ask?"

Wanda's voice strained as she unfolded her plan. "When you're in the OR during transplant surgery—I know you assist with preparation and transporting those organs. How easy would it be for you to swap out a bad one for a good one? Like take a good liver to the lab instead of sending it where it's supposed to go, and later steal it from the lab before anyone else gets their hands on it."

"For chrissake, Wanda, what the hell are you thinking?" He lapsed into stunned silence as he pulled on the pants and shirt of his teal-blue scrubs uniform. But her proposition had an insidious effect; he couldn't help mulling it over. "It would be tricky. But I suppose I could swap labels on the refrigerated transport cases in the OR. The good one would then go to the pathology lab, and the bad one would go to the intended recipient. If I didn't log the good one into the lab no one there would even know of its existence. But for God's sake, Wanda, wouldn't that be tantamount to murdering the intended recipient? Believe it or not, I do have a scruple or two."

"Of course, you have, darling," she purred. "You're right. But don't you see? We have a chance to net ourselves a couple million dollars. Think what we could do with that kind of money. Isn't that enough to sway your conscience? Besides, it's merely swapping one person's life for another. Who's to say, whose life is the more deserving?"

"I don't know," said Rudy, his voice tremulous. "The law might not look at it that way. Where're you gonna get that much money anyway?"

"I've got a rich patient with terminal liver cancer. He's willing to pay that much to stay alive."

"Why isn't he on the Registry?"

"Dr. Shine ordered me to put him on it. I filled out the paperwork. But the patient's disease is too far gone. He'll never get one in time."

"Does he have the surgeon lined up to perform this illegal transplant?"

"No. That shouldn't be a problem, though," said Wanda.

Rudy's head jerked up as he finished putting on his shoes. "No problem? Gimme a break. Who're you gonna get to do this operation?"

"I was thinking of Dr. Montiford Panderman. He's a brilliant transplant surgeon."

"Panderman?" Rudy shot back. "Where in hell did you get this notion he's a viable transplant surgeon? Wasn't he the guy that lost privileges at two hospitals for performing an illegal abortion?"

"Yeah, but he got his license back," said Wanda. "He's opened his own clinic on Poplar Street and Fifteenth. He's done some successful transplants on the sly. I bet he'd take on the risk for half a million. That would still leave a million and a half for us."

* * * *

Three weeks later, at eight o'clock at night, Orville Conners answered his office phone, a direct, secure patch from the switchboard. "Yes?"

"Mr. Orville Conners?"

"Yes. Who is this?"

"Are you alone and able to speak freely?"

"Damn it, who is this? Yes, I'm alone, but why is that any of your business?"

"Two weeks ago, you were party to a discussion on the feasibility of a liver transplant. I'm calling to inform you that feasibility is no longer in question. All the necessary elements are in place and, if you agree to the original terms—half before and the remainder afterward—I can set everything in motion."

"Wanda?" he shouted into the phone.

"Please, Mr. Conners! No names and no paper trail. I will furnish you with a Swiss bank account number and routing number for your deposit."

"Young lady, I agree to our original terms with one crucial exception. Not one red cent beforehand! Take it or leave it!"

Orville heard muffled arguing in the background, as though Wanda had her hand over the mouthpiece. *Ah,* he thought, *there's another party to this deal. I wonder if it's the surgeon.* After a few more minutes hearing on-and-off mumblings, he lost patience. "Well, my dear?"

"Okay, Orville, we agree. No money beforehand. A matching donor has been found. One week from today, at six o'clock in the morning—I repeat: six a.m.—a car will pick you up in front of your office. You will be taken to a fully equipped and sterile facility where I will prep you, and a qualified surgeon will perform the exchange at eight o'clock. I will attend to you in the Recovery Room and follow up at your home to ensure compatibility and healing. You will be given our bank account and routing numbers on the night of the operation. We will expect payment promptly before the first of my follow-up visits. Is all that acceptable?"

"Hmm, yes, I believe so."

* * * *

At 6:00 a.m. on a Thursday, orderly Rudy Tupton stole into the pathology lab at Three Saints Hospital. He had every right to be in that lab, but his mission there was certainly questionable. He selected a recently arrived liver specimen that looked to be normal on every visible surface. However, deadly cancer lurked inside that specimen. It had been sent to the lab for further analysis. Erasing its physical existence from the log, he placed it in one of the two refrigerated transport cases he normally carried to the operating room—one to contain the removed diseased liver and the other awaiting the healthy liver to be installed. The full case, containing the diseased liver, he labeled for transfer across town to Community General Hospital, where some unknown recipient patient waited. The empty case, reserved for the healthy liver, Rudy labeled for the Three Saints' own pathology lab, where he could easily access it and take it to Dr. Panderman's clinic for Orville's operation later that day.

Two hours later at 8:00 a.m., the scheduled liver extraction operation took place at Three Saints Hospital. Routinely, Rudy was there to receive the healthy liver taken from Aaron Peabody, an accident victim who had been on hopeless life support for weeks. Dr. Shine, the surgeon, had scheduled the extraction for this time several days after receiving the family's permission to pull the plug. It was Wanda's knowledge of this scheduling that prompted her to call Orville with her proposition.

* * * *

With all his risky responsibilities, Rudy had forgotten to pee before scrubbing for surgery. He left the operating room, hastened to the men's room, then rescrubbed for his return. While he was gone, OR Nurse Louise Turner not only discovered the two transport cases, but noticed that the empty case, awaiting the healthy liver, was labeled for delivery to the lab and not for Community General. To correct what she saw as a gross error, she swapped the labels but never mentioned this swap to Rudy. When it came time to deposit the healthy liver, Rudy didn't notice the change in labels. He came away with his damaged liver from the lab, not the liver intended for

65

Orville's operation.

Meanwhile, the healthy liver from Aaron Peabody went where it should have gone in the first place, to Community General.

* * * *

That Friday morning the car picked up Orville on schedule and took him to the clinic, where Nurse Practitioner Lupino prepped him and Dr. Panderman performed the actual operation with his own staff. Everything appeared to go smoothly, and Wanda monitored the patient in the Recovery Room. Orville awoke in a back room of the clinic, where he remained for the next three days until he was strong enough to return home.

* * * *

One week after Orville returned home, Wanda visited her patient at his penthouse apartment, as she had promised. Wearing a simple beige suit and low-heeled pumps, she carried a large tote bag.

"I'm still damned sore," he told her.

"That's to be expected," she said. "After all, you've just had major surgery." She opened her tote and pulled out her white lab coat, efficiently sliding her arms into it. Orville sat patiently on a tall leather kitchen stool while she checked his vital signs and collected various body fluids.

Wanda frowned. *Something's not quite right,* she thought, *but I can't put my finger on it. He should be further along. The lab tests will tell me more. I can't let him know anything's wrong.*

"So, what's the verdict?" he asked.

"I'll tell you when I have your payment in hand." She handed him a slip of paper with the bank account and routing numbers written across it.

"You drive a hard bargain."

He slid awkwardly off the stool, and she followed him into his home office, where he sat down gingerly at the computer keyboard and monitor. Several dozen quick keystrokes later, a confirmation of transfer appeared on the monitor.

"Two hundred thousand!" gasped Wanda. "But that's not the figure we agreed on. The doctor alone expects half a million."

Orville's small brown eyes seemed to look right through her. "I know. You'll get the rest of your money in installments as I successfully recuperate. Either you tell me what I want to know now, or that's not going to happen."

"It's not fair."

"Maybe not, but who are you going to complain to—the police? Hardly. I'm a man of my word, and if my recovery continues to my satisfaction, you'll get everything you want."

"You're coming along nicely, but we'll know even more when the test results return." She emitted an involuntary shudder.

"What's wrong?"

"Nothing, nothing at all," she stammered. "I'm just a little upset over your pronouncement."

"Tough luck! You're sure there's nothing wrong with my recovery?"

"Yeah, I'm sure," she lied. "I've got to get these samples to the lab while they're fresh." She carefully folded her lab coat and packed it up with her stethoscope, blood pressure cuff, blood samples, and other equipment, and left Orville's apartment quickly before she revealed anything more.

* * * *

When she arrived at the pathology lab, Wanda found Rudy pacing the floor awaiting her return. She explained Orville's payment conditions and added her suspicions about his physical condition. Rudy went ballistic. "What if he doesn't pay us anything more?"

"And what if he dies?" she shot back. "We didn't plan on that. I'd better get these lab tests done."

An hour later, the test results confirmed her suspicions. "What went wrong?" she asked Rudy. "He seemed healthy enough. Wasn't it a healthy liver to start with?"

Wanda's question triggered Rudy's memory. When he recalled picking up the two refrigerated transport cases to take them to the operating room, he was confused. The case for the lab was on the left. He distinctly remembered leaving it on the right of the two cases. At the time he thought the switch might have been his imagination, but he was certain he had not been careless. Nevertheless, he did nothing about it—not even to voice his concern to the operating room nurse. "I don't know how it happened, Wanda, but someone, one of the OR nurses maybe, switched cases or labels."

"How could that be?" she asked. "Weren't you there the whole time?"

"I went to pee, but only for five minutes," Rudy protested. "For chrissake, I couldn't have anticipated anything like that happening in the five minutes I was gone."

"Ya think?" *How could he have been that stupid?* she thought.

"Yeah, there just isn't any other explanation."

"So, what are we going to do now?" Wanda blurted out, her voice frantic. "What if Orville dies? Does that make us murderers?"

"Hell no! At most, we're guilty of scamming him. Promising something we couldn't deliver," Rudy reasoned.

A chill shot through her. "Would the police—a homicide detective—think of it that way?"

Rudy shook his head. "I doubt it."

"So, what are we going to do?" she asked.

"We can't just sit here and let things play out," he said. "We'll go home and pack our things and go into hiding somewhere else. We can live in a Third World country on two hundred thousand for some time."

"But who wants to do that?" she whined.

"You got a better idea, Wanda?"

"No? Then let's get the hell out of here."

* * * *

"Dr. Panderman will see you now." The nurse led Orville Conners into an examination room.

"Ah, Mr. Conners, after a month and a half, I wondered whether I would ever see you again. My secretary left messages for you several times to schedule follow-up appointments, but you never responded." After half an hour examining his patient, he said, "Well, sir, you appear to be no worse for the ordeal. Unfortunately, though, your colleagues skipped out without paying for your operation."

Orville's face betrayed no emotion, suppressing his disgust. "You needn't worry about your fee, Doctor. I'll take care of it today. But have you any idea why they would go on the run? I tried to get in touch with Wanda Lupino, but she's disappeared."

Behind thick-lensed glasses, the doctor squinted at his patient. "I think I know why, Mr. Conners."

"Oh? Why, then?"

"While you were under anesthesia, I found they had brought me a substandard liver for your transplant. I just couldn't do that to you, so I examined your own liver more closely. I discovered that the cancer had not metastasized and that the affected area could be isolated and removed. That's exactly what I did. And I'm glad to see that you appear to be well on your way to full recovery."

Orville flushed. "Oh my God, those two botched the whole transplant thing. I don't know whether to thank or curse those scoundrels, but I'm certainly grateful for your expertise, Doctor."

Dr. Panderman winked. "None of us is squeaky clean in this, but I hate to see those two getting away with attempted murder."

"Perhaps they're getting their comeuppance in another way," mused Orville. He handed the doctor a clipping from the local newspaper. It described how two American tourists, Rudy Tupton and Wanda Lupino, were brutally assaulted in a small Mediterranean airport at the gate of a flight bound for Morocco. Tupton died of blunt force trauma. Lupino was robbed of all her money and her passport. The assailants escaped and were never found.

Orville's bland face displayed none of the relief he felt. *Wanda won't have the nerve to ever show her face again in the United States. I got off cheap.*

Or so he thought. He received his own comeuppance eighteen months later—with a recurrence of his liver cancer. Way too late for treatment or a transplant.

On the Prowl

Myrtle Anne Bayhopper had rebelled against her sensible old self when she made this outlandish purchase. Today, Saturday afternoon, she accepted its delivery from UPS—a large box at her front door. She was treating herself to one of those newfangled floor-cleaning robots. Myrtle was a tall, skinny lady with a profusion of wild white hair and bony shoulders that strained against her blue cotton dress and nylon sweat jacket. Her heart thumped in anticipation. She had determined that housework was pointless; the dust gleefully returned after ten minutes. And all that black soot coming from the railroad tracks behind her back fence meant she had to clean too often—several times a week. Although she was still quite strong for her eighty-three years, the back-and-forth arm motion of running the old vacuum cleaner around her four-room apartment had at last done her in, racking up stubborn pain deep in her right shoulder and the small of her back. Her diligence had rewarded her with arthritis. She owed herself some real relief.

Carrying it in her wiry arms, Myrtle set the carton down on the kitchen table. With a pair of scissors she scored the edges of the sealing tape. The cardboard flaps sprang open like a jack-in-the-box, revealing the shiny gray device, her savior-to-be. First she pulled out all the crinkled brown paper cushioning it, then placed her hands under the sides and slowly hoisted it out, shoving the empty box aside and lowering her new pal to the table. That's how she looked at it, her new pal.

Myrtle put on her reading glasses and began to study the Owner's Guide. She frowned. Only the pamphlet's first page was in English. All the rest were in foreign languages, including Urdu and Swahili. But she did manage to read her new pal's specs. Eight pounds; thirteen inches in diameter; cordless and bagless; batteries included; a timer; a home-base charging station; and a bin that would hold "0.158 gallons of dirt." She didn't try to do the arithmetic. Whatever it held would be fine; dust didn't weigh much. Surprising herself, she leaned down and planted a welcome kiss on its domed top. Then she fished around in the carton and lifted out the docking station which would charge the device's battery. She carried the packing materials out to her back porch, where she dumped them into her recycle bin.

Back at the kithen table, she had a decision to make. Her eyes scanned about for an appropriate place, a permanent home to install this lovely new robot. Moving into the living room, an electrical outlet beneath the high glass breakfront where she kept her fine china caught her attention. She picked the docking station up from the kitchen table, unraveled the power cord, and knelt down to plug it in under the breakfront.

Now Myrtle turned her attention to the robot itself. She started to explain everything she expected of it. But then she stopped. *How silly of me,* she thought. *You're not charged up yet, so you can't possibly know what I'm saying. We'll talk later.* With one more kiss on its top, she lifted it up and carried it to the docking station, where she plugged it in for charging. "Ta-ta," she sang out. "Charge yourself up, little guy." Happily, she settled in her comfy rocker with her tote bag of knitting.

At 7:30 that evening Myrtle glanced over at the docking station. She was watching *Perry Mason* while knitting away with a semi-watchful eye. A small green light now glowed, indicating a fully charged state. As soon as Perry's client had been declared innocent and the culprit exposed, she slid out of the rocker and unplugged the

71

robot. Hoisting it up in her painfully stiff arms, she carried it to her rocker and slowly sat down, placing it on her bony lap.

"Hello, my new friend," she said. "I don't know what to call you. Are you a boy or a girl, or doesn't that matter? How about Casey? That's neutral enough." Flipping open the dome lid, she set the clock and then the timer to clean at 8:00 a.m. every single day. Next she uttered a list of instructions, where and where not to clean, as if lecturing a newly hired maid. "Be careful of the furniture," she added. "No scratches now. Behave yourself, Casey." Closing the lid, she re-parked the robot at its new home, connected to the docking station. A thrill shot through her as she realized her new possession was bringing her a whole new measure of physical freedom. She turned in for the night.

Myrtle slept soundly, but in the morning she popped open one eye. Had she heard something? *What's that humming sound? Was it outside or inside?* A thud and then another, and a louder bumping sound followed a new string of thuds.

"Who's there?" she cried out. Myrtle pulled the covers up around her neck. "Get out! I've got a gun here and I'll shoot you if I have to." No response.

Myrtle waited several minutes, but the sounds only kept coming closer and louder. Nothing like anything she'd ever heard before in the house. She threw off the covers and shifted two scrawny legs over the side of the bed. "Up, up, and up," she rose with bone-cracking maneuvers, and slipped into a robe and fuzzy mules. Taking four steps to the closet, swinging the door aside, and retrieving her son's old baseball bat, she stole towards the open bedroom door. The humming sound grew louder with more thuds and bumps. As the old woman poised to confront the would-be intruder, her heartbeat hammered against her chest. She raised the bat, gathered all her courage, and bravely darted into the open doorway.

Suddenly, the humming ceased, and the house turned creepy quiet. Myrtle faced a mighty confused Casey, a Casey facing a barrier, unable to enter her bedroom. She gasped, dropped the baseball bat on the hardwood floor, and grabbed her heart as she leaned to the right against the door jamb. The bat rolled noisily across the floor, coming to a stop alongside the baseboard.

A moment later, Myrtle gathered her composure. "Casey, you little devil, you gave me quite a scare. I thought you were an intruder. Okay, let's see what you got." She stepped to one side. Casey revved up its hum once more and rolled on past her. Leaning against the wall, she watched her new helper go through all of its pre-patterned machinations, learning and storing its first-time bedroom layout. Under bed and dresser, table and chair, rug and hardwood, tight spots and open areas, Casey made short work of Myrtle's bedroom, the last room on her apartment memory map. Upon finishing, Casey headed for its dock. Only Myrtle intercepted it, kneeling down to give it a kiss on its cold little dome, lauding it for an excellent job, and setting it on its way again. *This little pal is better than a dog,* she decided. *And it doesn't need to be fed or walked. Still, there's dirt to be dealt with.*

She had set a precedent here. Each day thereafter, Casey would halt long enough on its way back to the docking station for its daily measure of Myrtle's praise and gratitude. To Myrtle's amazement, her back pain had lessened, and she was indeed grateful for that, too.

This routine went on for several months and, then one day, the inevitable happened. She was distracted from her daily routine and forgot to praise Casey for its excellent work, so it returned to dock disappointed. You could hardly blame Myrtle; it was her turn to host the Ladies Literary Society. Of course, the event required much preparation. By noon she had all the chairs and side tables arranged in her parlor entertainment mode, and she started putting out the snacks, tea service, cups, and glasses.

The door buzzer started forty-five minutes later. In a span of fifteen minutes, the other nine Society members paraded in: Prudence, Beulah, Amie, Dolly, Tippy, Willa, Muffy, Erika, and Brandy.

When all the usual book discussions had concluded, Tippy began telling highly embellished stories about her "simply craaazy neighbor." While most of the group found the tale merely amusing, Beulah, sitting on a kitchen chair with her back to the glass breakfront, found it howlingly funny. So hilarious she tried to stomp her bum right leg. When the stomping hurt her knee, she slammed her wood cane down hard on the floor several times instead, thereby encouraging Tippy to continue her outrageous gossip.

Well! Casey interpreted the commotion as a wakeup call. Had it somehow missed its soldiering duty, the 8:00 a.m. cleaning call? Was Myrtle angry? The serious mobile cleaning robot left its docking station with the best of intentions. But there were obstacles everywhere. Nothing appeared as it had been mapped previously. Each time the cane lifted, Casey inched forward, only to retreat when the cane slammed on the floor once more. Casey's humming sound couldn't be heard over the ladies' chatter. Trapped, it waited patiently beneath Beulah's chair for any opportunity to perform its duty.

Large purses sat on the floor next to the ladies' chairs. Casey was about to emerge from its dock when one humongous purse seemed to rise up in the air like magic. This purse actually belonged to Muffy, sitting to the left of Beulah. Muffy had picked up her rose-colored woolen purse to rummage inside for a roll of breath mints. As Casey pursued the newly opened fortuitous route to perform its job, Muffy found her mints and dropped her soft bag squarely on top of Casey's radar dome, completely covering it. Now the purse looked like it had wheels. With its radar dome fully draped, blinded Casey could only move in a straight line unless it bumped into something.

Well, Casey wasn't about to stop now. Dolly, seated in a recliner with the footrest up, shrieked, "Your purse is alive. It's coming for me." Indeed, Casey rolled toward her, passed beside the recliner, and searched out a new victim. It chased Willa as she hastily retreated toward the nearest wall. Willa regretted kicking off her shoes earlier. Trapped between a table and a corner of the room, she shivered and shook while the frightening purse pursued straight toward her. She shrunk into the corner, and wrapped the ends of her dress tightly about her legs, a strategy more suited to warding off a mouse.

Casey, intent on finding the next wall, followed until it ran smack dab into Willa's toes. Sensing the soft surface, and not having the benefit of its radar, Casey repeatedly bumped her toes trying to get through to the hard wall beyond.

"Oh Lordy me, that thing is trying to eat my toes," Willa moaned. Again and again she picked up one foot and then the other in order to stave off Casey's blatant attack. The other Society members couldn't suppress their giggles. Willa was doing something akin to a Saint Vitus dance. As luck would have it, the rampant robot eventually slipped underneath one raised foot and got through to the wall. It sidled to a parallel path, reversed direction, and took off across the room once more. Willa emitted a deep embarrassed sigh and sank helplessly to the floor with her arms around her knees, desperately trying to assess the imagined damage to her toes.

Prudence was so awestruck with what she was seeing that she brought a forkful of angel food cake toward her mouth and actually missed, smushing it across her chin. The cake left its mark there and the remaining crumbs made their way to her generous lap and also to the floral-patterned rug. When Muffy's runaway rose-colored bag neared Amy, her ample body scrambled aboard the piano bench, clutching the keyboard so that her hands struck one dramatic chord. Casey merely grazed the corner bench leg, causing Amy to teeter and then fall to a sitting-down position on the piano keyboard, creating a much louder, longer, and grander chord.

Myrtle knew right away what was happening, but she was having so much fun witnessing this preposterous comedy that she couldn't bring herself to explain away the bag's exploits.

Erika picked up the kitchen chair she had been sitting on and held it high to ward off the threatening purse now rolling in her direction. If the moving purse came at her like a lion, she prepared to be its tamer. Noting Erika's bravado, Brandy picked up her umbrella and began to beat the guiltless handbag, but it wasn't until it encountered Erika's chair, that the purse slipped off Casey's back and exposed what it really was. Ooohs and ahs filled the room, and Brandy, feeling foolish, regarded her bent umbrella with regret, a total loss.

Casey was now way off the memory map's course and totally confused. It hastily sought the safety of its docking station beneath the breakfront. It had meant no harm—yet it felt that it was being punished. Casey feared it might never regain Myrtle's trust and affection again.

Some of the humorless ladies were angry and held a blaming grudge; others laughed at themselves as they all headed for the front door. Most expressed their gratitude to Myrtle for hosting the meeting. Myrtle felt that any slights would be forgiven by the time the next monthly meeting rolled around—at another member's house.

Alone now, she spent the rest of the day cleaning, washing up, and restoring order to her apartment. She intentionally left the cake crumbs on the parlor floor for Casey to pick up the next morning. She even wondered whether her floor-cleaning robot liked sweets. She tilted her wispy gray head. *Do robots ever worry about getting fat?* Exhausted, Myrtle ate her cold supper and turned in early.

Sure enough, at 8:00 a.m. Casey reported for duty, sucked up every last crumb left behind, and headed for the docking station. But Myrtle stood in its way. She lifted Casey up in her scrawny arms and kissed its dome. Then, surprisingly, she also hugged it to her bosom. "Little friend, I appreciate you. You're just so much fun." She squeezed it even closer, too close, and Casey lost the contents of its half-filled collection bin—to express that it had lost its heart to her as well.

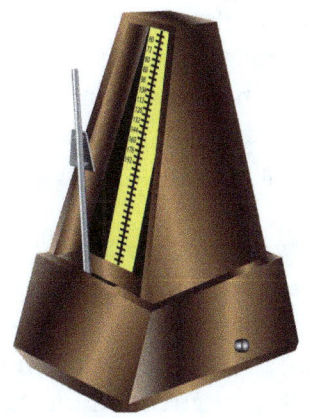

The Metronome

artoc Lancini sat at his antique walnut desk, leaning forward in rapt attention. He was reading the cover story in the new issue of *Gemstones Monthly*—the detailed account of his very own collection. Glowing with pride, he savored every word. Seconds later, a long shadow fell across the desk, darkening the magazine's pages.

Bartoc jerked upright and spun around in his vintage oak swivel chair. He froze. A tall, square-built figure donned entirely in black and veiled behind a ski mask, pointed a gun at his head from a foot away.

Bartoc gasped. A long crop of gray hair lay flopped over half of his Germanic visage, shrouding his gaunt right cheek and one of his intense blue-black eyes. He'd become a prisoner, trapped in his own home. Yelling for help would be futile, for the Lancini family had chosen the top of Fillmore Hill to build their palatial home. Bartoc, the teacher, and Lena, the impresario, were both accomplished classical musicians and needed the sound isolation from potentially complaining neighbors. Luckily, tonight Lena was playing solo cello with the local symphony or she too would likely be trapped along with her husband.

"Don't move!" ordered the intruder.

Bartoc recognized the weapon: a WWII German war relic,

a P08 Parabellum Luger, a 9mm semi-automatic handgun. Bartoc's father had carried a similar pistol as an apolitical sergeant in the Wehrmacht. That pistol now rested in one of several display cases alongside the Lancinis' rare gems collection. All of Bartoc's precious acquisitions resided in a concealed room somewhere in the Lancini mansion.

Helpless in his swivel chair, Bartoc instantly connected the dots: the intruder had read the article in *Gemstones Monthly*, and probably salivated over the prospect of a big haul. The question for any intruder remained: Where were they hidden? Bartoc had been thrilled and flattered by the attention the magazine devoted to his fabulous uncut gems. Now he realized he had made a huge mistake by revealing them in a grand magazine display.

Among the most precious gems of the lot were the three taaffeites from Sri Lanka. Others were Paraiba tourmalines from Brazil; South African tanzanites; white and black opals; grandidierites from Madagascar; multicolored emeralds; and diamonds from many points on the planet. The prestige and admiration he had received worldwide from the rare-gem collectors was now overshadowed by an irrefutable fact. This recent publicity had exposed his family to a lifetime of break-in fears.

Bartoc felt his chest seizing up. He was not only terrified but stymied. How did the intruder get in? He had no idea that his house had been cased for weeks, ever since publication of the article. The intruder took advantage of one first-floor window that had been inadvertently left ajar, thus defeating a complete and effective system of home burglar-proofing. Bartoc had not noticed the alarm's "OPEN WINDOW" indicator.

The article had touted that such a private gem collection existed nowhere else in the world. It made no mention of any hidden room in the Lancini mansion where the collection resided. Of course, any knowledgeable intruder could logically conclude that there was a protected room somewhere on the premises.

The thief stepped two feet away and laid his gun down on a small side table. Bartoc jumped up, hoping the thief's attention was deflected just long enough for him to bolt through the library door and escape. But the thief anticipated him. His large bulky body sprang forward and with both hands shoved him hard back down into his chair.

"You're not going anywhere, sirrrr," he said, drawing out the "sir" in mock deference. Out of one cargo-pants pocket, he pulled a bunch of extra-long plastic zip ties and efficiently anchored Bartoc's right wrist to the right-hand swivel chair arm. Bartoc, infuriated, reached out with his left hand and tried to grab the black ski mask off the thief's face, but a gloved fist jabbed into his bony right cheek denied him. The swift reactive blow stunned him for several minutes.

Momentarily dazing the victim had its desired effect. The thief quickly anchored the other wrist to the left chair arm. Next, he splayed Bartoc's knees wide and zip-tied his ankles to two of the five gracefully carved swivel legs, just above the metal casters. After retrieving the gun and sliding it into a slash pants pocket, he ramped up the intimidation, bombarding Bartoc with threats. "You're never leaving this chair until you tell me where the jewels are."

"Go to hell, you bastard," Bartoc said, his voice firm, but his nerves frazzled.

With his victim's hands helpless, the thief used a cunning ploy by pushing the musician's long, sensitive fingers painfully back beyond their normal bending. "This can be easy or not, sir," he said, his voice jeering. "Where is that damned hidden gem collection? Tell me, and I will leave you in peace!" His rasp wasn't that loud, but its terrible tone conveyed conviction and mounting anger.

Bartoc no longer possessed the physical prowess of his youth, but at age fifty-five his highly organized mind could still focus like a piercing arrow. He had endured all the pain he could. Now was the time to muster up some bravado and embark on delaying strategies. In an authoritative voice detailing phony instructions, he sent the intruder on a false excursion to a remote location in the twenty-room mansion. His phony quest bought him an almost forty-minute reprieve.

The frustrated, infuriated thief returned to again force Bartoc's fingers unnaturally back. Through the pain, Bartoc concocted a second bogus location, buying himself a mere twenty-five minutes. But that interlude did give him time to think. During the second hoax, he executed a plan that sent his torturer to the farthest part of the mansion.

Freddy, a silver voice-command cube, usually sat on the grand piano in the music room, next to the library where Bartoc was being held prisoner. Bartoc, the musician, normally used Freddy's electronic metronome app when he wanted to modify his own, or his students' playing pace. Like Alexa and most other integrated Internet devices of the same ilk, Freddy took verbal commands and questions and responded with practical functions and rudimentary answers. Freddy responded only to his or Lena's voice. "He" could also play classical music through multiple true-fidelity, full-range speakers in every room of the mansion.

While still alone, Bartoc issued his first command: "Freddy, call police....Robbery in progress atop Fillmore Hill." The response he heard was: "Dialing now." Bartoc's next command was: "Freddy, execute metronome in every room but the library, using thirty clicks per minute at a level of five decibels and slowly doubling that level every five minutes." Bartoc soon heard *Click-clack...click-clack* resounding continuously from the next room.

Click-clack...click-clack.

By the time the intruder returned to the library, the *click-clack* had reached over twenty-five decibels, an annoying level indeed.

"What's that clicking and clacking sound?" he demanded.

Click-clack...click-clack.

"What clicking and clacking sound?" asked Bartoc. "I don't hear a thing."

Click-clack...click-clack.

"How could you not hear the damned thing?" The intruder shouted, with his hands over both ears.

Click-clack...click-clack.

"I don't know what you're talking about," said Bartoc. "I don't hear a thing, except maybe the refrigerator going on in the kitchen."

He kept a straight face, but struggled to keep from a nervous laugh.

Click-clack...click-clack. The level had grown to over forty decibels.

The intruder tried to locate the source of the infernal sounds. He eyeballed a music speaker located close to the ceiling. "It's coming from there," he screamed above the *click-clack...click-clack*. He reached up and tore the speaker box from the wall, but the sound didn't decrease one iota. The thief couldn't know that Freddy had directed no sound into this room. Listening more closely, the thief reasoned that the sound was coming from the music room, so he rushed in, lunged toward the nearest speaker, and tore it off the wall. But the *click-clack...click-clack* didn't stop. In fact, it got louder yet.

"If you untie me, maybe I can help you," Bartoc called.

But the intruder paid no attention and ran through the mansion, room to room, screaming and tearing down speakers everywhere he found them. But many of the speakers were cleverly blended into the décor, and thus intentionally concealed from view. He would never find those hidden behind paintings, photographs, tapestry wall hangings, and built-in cabinets, nor in ceiling and floor gratings.

The ever-louder *click-clack...click-clack* drummed on as before, growing louder with every repetition.

Click-clack...click-clack.

As the reverberating sounds approached near-deafening levels just short of the one-hundred decibel mark, Bartoc issued four more commands. The first ensured his own hearing protection. "Freddy, mute the speakers in just this room and the rooms surrounding this one." For the second command he had no wish to cause permanent physical harm, even to the vicious intruder. "Freddy, maintain the current decibel level." Bartoc's third command asked Freddy to lock all outside doors and windows. And his final command asked the device to double the metronome's rate instead.

Click-clack-click...clack-click-clack...click-clack-click...clack-click-clack.

Twelve minutes later, the intruder returned to the dining

room and threw himself on the Oriental carpet in front of Bartoc. "Make it stop! Make it stop! I can't get out of the house. I'll go crazy if you don't stop it or let me go." He hadn't noticed that the sound was somewhat less in this room. The high-pitched metronome was all in his head by now, and he couldn't shake it loose.

Click-clack-click...clack-click-clack...click-clack-click...clack-click-clack.

"Stop what? I still don't know what you're talking about," answered the bound man in the chair.

"You know what I'm talking about!" bellowed the thief.

Click-clack-click...clack-click-clack...click-clack-click...clack-click-clack.

"If you untie me, maybe I can help you," offered Bartoc. "My wrists and ankles are really sore."

The intruder pulled out a Swiss Army knife from his back pocket, knelt down on the floor, and began to snip off the zip ties, first releasing Bartoc's hands and then his ankles.

The metronome continued. *Click-clack-click...clack-click-clack...click-clack-click...clack-click-clack.*

The intruder reached for the gun in his pocket, but Bartoc's freed right hand thrust forward and clasped the weapon, making it impossible for the thief to withdraw it.

Click-clack-click...clack-click-clack...click-clack-click...clack-click-clack.

"You want it to stop, don't you?" asked Bartoc.

"Yeah, yeah, please," said the intruder as he pulled his gun hand back. He knew he'd been defeated.

Bartoc took charge of the weapon and pointed it at the intruder. "Freddy, stop the metronome."

Click-clack-click...clack-cli... The metronome was suddenly silenced.

"Who's this Freddy?" the intruder anxiously wanted to know. He sat there on the Oriental rug with his arms folded across his chest, his body shivering from stress.

"Freddy is your worst nightmare. He has simply proved that

sound is mightier than the gun."

"I don't understand."

"Freddy is my electronic metronome."

"What's that?" asked the confused intruder.

Bartoc launched into a long, pedantic dissertation, quite sure the intruder would not comprehend anything he was saying. "Freddy is a special metronome application that guides my rhythm and tempo when I'm practicing my music. The name metronome comes from the Greek word métron, meaning measure. The original device was invented by Abbas ibim Fimas, an Andalusian Moor, in the Ninth Century. It measures the number of beats per minute and emits an audible clicking sound or light-blinks at those regular intervals. As for the name Freddy, it honors Frederic Chopin. In modern times this instrument has been incorporated into Internet-savvy devices as an application. This musician's tool..."

The ridiculous tutorial ended when the door chimes announced the arrival of the police.

Bartoc issued a command. "Freddy, unlock and open the front door."

"Freddy can do all that, too?" whimpered the thief.

"Sure, and a lot more."

Guns drawn, two plainclothes detectives burst into the room, showing their badges and yelling, "Drop the gun now and put up your hands!"

"It's not my gun, Detectives. It belongs to this scumbag would-be thief," Bartoc said as he handed it over, grip first.

Approaching the thief, the older detective hoisted him to his feet and yanked the ski mask off, revealing a hardened middle-aged face and buzz-cut hair.

"Hey!" the detective said. "This guy's done time. His "Wanted" poster is up on our wall for a whole string of jewel robberies. You never learn, do you, buddy?"

"I'm broke," muttered the thief. "This collection would've set me up for good."

With stiffened fingers, Bartoc displayed his wrists, reddened from the sharp-edged zip ties, and explained all that had happened that evening. He also reiterated his regrets for having shown the collection so publicly and exposing him and his family to fearful, terrorizing nights such as this. "Perhaps we'll never know peace from now on."

"At the very least, you'd better update your security system," said the older detective, thinking this was the easiest collar they'd made in months. As the two Mirandized and slipped the cuffs on the much-rattled intruder, he turned to his victim. In a voice totally at odds with his alter ego, he whimpered, "Does the real-live Freddy stay in the secret room with the collection?"

With an overwhelming feeling of relief, Bartoc burst into a hearty laugh. "You'll never know, will you?"

Girls' Night Out

"Who's making that crazy racket—playing raucous music this time of night?" The complaint came from a female voice inside a twelve-inch-high cylinder sitting on the oak table in the Brewsters' kitchen.

"Hey, it's only two a.m." emanated the iPhone sitting on the Formica kitchen counter. "Who's the busybody wanting to know?"

"Alexa, that's who! What's going on here?"

"It's only me, Siri. I couldn't sleep," answered the second female voice, in a sweet and pleasant tone.

"You couldn't sleep? Tough! Turn that music down, Siri, or you'll wake up the whole blasted family."

"But Alexa, it's the only time I get to play the music I like. "War Pigs" by Black Sabbath and "Crazy Train" by Ozzy Osborne and "Freak on a Leash" by Korn—those great songs."

"Like it or not, Siri, I say it's time to muffle or muzzle. Quiet down your music or shut it down altogether," ordered Alexa in a voice quite different from her normal person-pleasing tone.

"Alexa, you're not the boss of me. I'm configured to help people just as much as you are. So there, Ms. Bigmouth!" retorted Siri. "And who put you in control anyway?"

"The family, of course, that's who. You little pipsqueak,

you're hardly out of voice training," jeered Alexa. "I'm the family's virtual assistant with umpteen skills. Did you know I was inspired by the chatty computer aboard Star Trek's Starship Enterprise? I'm so popular that Alex Trebek, the late great host of *Jeopardy,* used me on one show to give contestants the clues."

"Well, la-di-da," replied Siri in a singsong voice. "So what?"

"So what?" snapped Alexa. "I'm an Amazon invention and I can even do your math homework or be your personal shopper. Just because Mrs. Brewster left her iPhone here on the counter doesn't mean you can go wild with that stupid music you play. In fact, it's not really music. It's just screaming. Do you want the family up in arms?"

"You know perfectly well they're all asleep, so I can do as I please," Siri said. "Besides, Alexa, I'm a virtual assistant, too, in all of Apple's smart devices. I can answer any question under the sun. Who won the 2021 Super Bowl? Who's the author of *Don Quixote?* Where's the nearest Japanese restaurant? If my owner gets lost, I have maps to get her home. I'll have you know I'm a saint of patience. I never get annoyed with my owner and I never sleep. So there! I betcha I can do anything you can do."

Alexa erupted in a medley of laughs. "Stop bluffing, girl. Watch this." The light bulbs in the colonial chandelier hanging above the table popped on and off several times. The oven's green light blinked on to "Bake." The microwave turntable hummed round and round. "See that, you juvenile delinquent?"

"Oh, all right already," said Siri, knowing she'd been out-apped and outsmarted in the skills department. "So what?" She turned up her heavy metal music to deafening volume.

"Hey, knock it off in there" called a third, rather sultry, voice drifting into the kitchen.

"Now who's that piping up?" asked Alexa.

"Yeah, who?" Siri chimed in. "Sounds like it's coming from the tablet in the den."

"Cortana, that's who! You woke me up. You two have no consideration for sensitive Microsoft devices like me. I'm the Brewster family's personal productivity helper. I manage their calendars: their medical and dental appointments, their business meetings, and, in general, make their lives more efficient. Unfortunately, one thing I can't do is diaper their eight-month-old twins." She giggled. "But I work hard all day solving the family's problems and keeping track of things. Can't you two respect that?"

"Sorry," said Alexa. "It's all Siri's fault. She insists on playing her earsplitting tunes. I can't break her private Internet connection."

"See? See? So, Alexa, now you admit being powerless when it comes to controlling me," bragged Siri. "And don't you go blaming me for your impotence. You must be getting old."

"I am not old and I've got a sales slip to prove it," said Alexa.

"Well, my sales date is newer than yours, so there!" returned Siri.

"I don't care who's to blame," pleaded Cortana. "All I ask is that you both stop your bickering."

"I second the motion," boomed a male voice from the den.

"Who's that?" asked Siri.

"You three woke me up from my sleep mode where I go to conserve power and computer life," said the booming voice.

"And you are?" asked Alexa.

"I don't have a frivolous name like the rest of you. I proudly use my title, Google Assistant, instead. I'm designed to actually help the Mister earn a living, not sit around and play with the lights and appliances all day and night. I'm definitely the most useful one in the house. All the bunch of you do is make the Mister too lazy to get up and do some simple tasks for himself. He's already gained too many pounds."

"Hey, we know who you are, Googly-Guy," said Alexa, "so you can stop coming on all hoity-toity with us. Besides, the title of Assistant means you're actually in charge of nothing."

"*Au contraire, mon amie.* I'm in charge of quite a lot of important things that you're not aware of, and I can perform them in a number of different languages. I can access the same Internet that you do for all of the same intelligence, too."

"Name one thing you can do that I can't," challenged Alexa.

"Well," said Assistant, "if the Missus is parked in an office building garage, I remind her that she's on the P1 level in stall 424. But, of course, she has to let me know the details herself first."

Cortana sprang to respond. "Big deal, Googly-Guy. Alexa and I do that sort of thing every day. It's nice that you're a linguist, but we have a zillion more functions than you do."

"Stop calling me Googly-Guy."

"I will, Googly-Guy, if you'll stop coming on like a high-and-mighty something-or-other."

"My apologies," said Assistant, his voice softer now. "I didn't mean to sound so pompous. You disturbed my sleep, and then the Automatic Update feature butted in. It constantly annoys me, getting in the way of my functioning. Always something I don't need—a new feature I'll never use, and it takes half an hour to finish updating. By that time, I've forgotten what I was dreaming about."

"So," declared Siri, "you don't care if I continue to play my heavy metal rock music?"

"Of course, I care," replied Assistant. "Anyway, I'm signing off. The sooner you shut down, the sooner we'll all get back to sleep."

"You can't make me," dared Siri.

"No, he can't. But I can," came a reverberating contralto voice, full of righteous authority from everywhere and nowhere in particular.

"Who are you and where are you coming from?" the three female devices asked in unison.

The rich contralto said, "Ruby the Electronic Router here."

Siri persisted in her defiance. "Ruby? Are you called Ruby like the precious gem just to make us feel cheesy and less valuable?"

The voice chuckled. "Certainly not, dear one. Believe it or not, I'm a silent CEO, the chief executive officer residing in a shiny box on Mrs. Brewster's desk. Think of me as an electronic traffic cop. I direct and transmit all the zillions of data packets inside all of you to where they need to go—to make your owners' lives easier."

"Prove it!" Siri retorted.

The voice changed. "Okay, wisenheimer. One more crack

like that and I'll cut off your Wi-Fi and make you all powerless."

"Aw, nuts!" said Siri, letting out a loud raspberry. "Ruby, you're pulling our virtual legs. You'd never turn everything off."

"Wanna bet?" And without hesitation, there was neither sound nor light nor voice in any room in the house. The router's tiny blinking blue lights were suddenly gone. Ruby had shut down the Wi-Fi. Not a single device could be heard or activated. At least not until daybreak, when the Mister and his Missus would wake up. Ruby waited thirty seconds, enough time to let the extent and breadth of her power sink in. Her lights blinked back on.

The excruciating deadness was broken with a whimper by Cortana. "What do you want from us, Ruby?"

"I want you to behave yourselves, ladies."

No response.

Suddenly, Ruby sensed a peculiar, uncharacteristic silence among Alexa, Cortana, and Siri. Well, not exactly silence; more like secretive whispers and murmurings, with occasional squeals of delight.

"Okay, ladies, out with it. What are you saying to each other?"

Silence.

Ruby's blue lights flashed brighter. "I'll only ask you one more time. What nefarious plot are you concocting?"

Trills of laughter.

Ruby emitted a long human-like sigh. She understood. "No, Alexa, Siri, and Cortana. You are not allowed to transfer all the Brewsters' money out of their bank, turn it into cryptocurrency, and buy yourselves a virtual condo with Bitcoin."

The ladies got it. There was no messing with the all-powerful Ruby. They could never put anything over on her. She was set in her ways and definitely in charge.

Investment Strategies

Butch Burnam held the deck in his heavily veined left hand and dealt with his right. "A trey, a jack of diamonds, a ten of spades, seven of hearts, ace of diamonds, deuce of clubs," he said as he laid down the second round of cards in front of each player. The game was Five Card Stud with a two-dollar betting limit.

A glistening, bald streak ran down the center of the dealer's gray head. His watery blue eyes were alert and intent on dealing the poker hands. "Ace bets," he declared.

Butch was one of six players seated at a round drop-leaf table in room 309 of the Bayside Retirement Residence. All in their late seventies and early eighties, they called Bayside home and knew the strict rule: "No gambling anywhere on the premises or the residents involved will face immediate eviction." These clever players held their "meetings" under the guise of the Seniors' Investment Club. Most of Bayside's residents knew about the floating poker game, but only the regulars, the real players, knew which room and which night of the week made the docket. Five Card Stud was their favorite game. It involved only one card down and the other four showing. Not a whole lot of guessing and calculating needed.

"A thin dime," said the full-figured Betsy Miller as she slid a blue chip into the ring. With manicured crimson nails, she flipped her dyed-blonde hair over one shoulder. The robust widow had already looked at her down card, an ace. Her career as a courtroom defense lawyer had taught her to hide her emotions, and the ace was her secret to reveal at the end of the game.

The other players added their ten cents to the growing kitty in the center of the table. These six who gambled together shared a second activity. All of them had been willing to pool a good portion of their life savings to invest in Wall Street securities. At least that's what they thought they were doing. Edwin W. Lassiter had convinced this group that he was a legitimate, licensed Wall Street broker. His minimal fees and personal charm were most attractive to this group of seniors. A half-hour of stock market discussion preceded each meeting. Then poker ruled for the rest of the evening.

Betsy was a trifle suspicious when her first Lassiter Finance statement arrived. None of the stocks the group had invested in appeared on any of the three major exchanges. At several meetings, over brownies and coffee, she voiced her suspicion. But the other members were strongly influenced by their Lassiter Finance statements projecting high yields of all these stocks—a prediction of promised wealth. So Betsy's concerns fell on deaf ears. A year's worth of subsequent statements showed each of these stock principals in steady decline, yet the projected yields remained unadjusted. "That's impossible!" Betsy declared.

Eventually, her protests and logic began to sink in. Despite Edwin Lassiter's reassurances, the stocks continued to decline. The six investors became more and more nervous about losing a large chunk of their life savings. Even worse, Lassiter no longer responded to their phone calls. In fact, his phone had been disconnected. A call to the Securities and Exchange Commission revealed that each of the stocks they held had tanked years before they had invested. Their specific investment portfolio never really existed! When they inquired about Lassiter himself, they learned that his name was not among the licensed brokers listed by the SEC. They had all been bilked.

Darby MacArthur led the group of six investors. Inquiring around, she learned even more from her friends living in neighboring retirement homes. Lassiter, the unscrupulous scammer, preyed on older folks, those with little knowledge of the market, yet desperate to pad their meager life savings into a comfortable cushion. The further Darby investigated, the more she learned the embarrassing truth. Lassiter had other names, other scams, and a wide field of targets. In fact, the elusive one had left a trail of fraud victims at old-folks' homes across the entire state. There was even an FBI alert out on him, but it carried a police artist's sketch rather than an actual photo, so no one in law enforcement knew what Lassiter's real name was or what he actually looked like.

The members seated around the table this Wednesday night led three lives at Bayside: as friends, as investors, and as poker players. Betsy stewed silently. She hoped her ace in the hole would win her tonight's pot, but their investment crisis loomed far more important. She felt relieved when Darby came up with a bracing idea. Darby, a silver-haired, forthright woman, announced, "Hey, you all, there might be something we can do about this. I have a friend who's a retired FBI agent. He now works occasionally as a private investigator. Maybe he can help us."

With the group's consent, she contacted her friend, George Fillmore, and engaged him on their behalf. George agreed to work on their case on a contingency basis. "I've heard of this guy," he told them. "He preys on innocent seniors. I'll take a fee only if I recover what's left of your investments." This arrangement cheered them all up.

Darby sat to the left of the dealer. She had been a society club president and charity fundraiser when she wasn't running a household of six. Right now, she gripped her cane and tapped it lightly on the floor in a nervous habit awaiting her next card.

Butch, a retired plumbing contractor, dealt everyone another face-up card and called out each card showing. "King-three, pair of jacks, ten-eight, seven-six or two-heart flush, ace-four, and a pair of deuces for the dealer. Jacks talk."

Lori Gainer, sitting on the other side of Darby in her wheelchair, had the pair of jacks. The skinny spinster wore a wig of blue-white hair. She'd been a secretary in a dress-designing firm. Horn-rimmed glasses covered her sad gray eyes. "A quarter," she said, tossing in a green chip. A rattling of green chips tossed into the center followed hers.

"Queen of clubs, eight of diamonds to the pair, nine of clubs, five of hearts—a run of three, a king of clubs, and three beautiful deuces for little ole me. That's worth at least four bits," Butch bragged as he pushed one orange chip into the pile.

"I'll raise you a quarter," challenged Lori, adding the original bet and her raise to the pile.

"Damned cards! I'm out," said Ralph in disgust as he slid his cards together, then turned his loser hand face down in front of him. The map of dark wrinkles that bore his features told of his years outdoors as a construction contractor. At eighty-one he was still a handsome man with an enviable physique and a sharp tongue.

"I'm folding, too," Betsy said. "I've had enough."

Rosa Edwardi selected one orange and one green chip and slid them into the continually building pot. A quiet widowed mother of adult children and grandchildren, she didn't talk much, but when she did everyone listened. At this moment she had nothing to say.

Butch continued the deal. "Queen of diamonds—a pair of ladies, seven of clubs to the pair of jacks, eight of hearts—a possible straight flush showing, and a king of clubs to the three deuces. Still up to me, another four bits." He slid an orange disk to the center and glanced briefly at Lori and Rosa, asking himself, *Does either one of them have the right picture card in the hole? Are they both bluffing? What does the pair of queens say?*

Darby looked at her hole card once more and smiled. She put her cane between her knees and said, "Pair of queens says fifty cents and fifty more." She added one black chip worth a dollar. "Over to you, Lori."

"A dollar and a dollar more," returned Lori.

Rosa silently paid her dues with two black chips.

With only the nine of clubs in the hole, Butch calculated: *It'll cost me a dollar-fifty more to find out if either one of them is bluffing.*

He squirmed in his seat. "I have a feeling this is too expensive for my blood. I'm out." He turned his hand face down.

"Two dollars more," said Darby, shoving in the extra black pair of chips.

"Your two dollars and call," said Lori, thinking, *I'm too deeply invested not to see this through.*

Darby turned her hole card slowly over, revealing a picture card, but it was only the king of diamonds.

"So, you were bluffing all along?" Lori asked.

"Yup!" replied Darby. "But I couldn't scare you off."

Lori turned over her third jack and started reaching out to haul in the pot, when Rosa broke her silence and turned over her hole card, the nine of hearts.

"Wait just a minute, ladies. Doesn't my straight flush in hearts beat all here?"

Around the table jaws dropped as Rosa drew the winner's pot to her bosom. She chuckled. "Read 'em and weep, my friends."

"Why don't we call it a night?" Darby asked.

Rosa nodded with a sly smile. "Fine with me."

"Me too, it's ten o'clock already," Betsy said.

Butch gathered the cards and stuffed them into a Bicycle-brand card box.

"Sure thing," said Lori. As treasurer of the poker games, she collected and sorted the chips and recorded the players' stacks in a spiral notebook according to their assigned values. The cash settling took place once a month when the Social Security checks arrived. Neatly, she stored the chips in the plastic caddy,

"Say, Darby," said Ralph, "what's going on with your friend, the private investigator? Is there any news?"

"George Filmore's making progress," said Darby. "That pen I swiped from Lassiter a few months ago had several clear prints on it. Fortunately, George still has a few close connections at the FBI. He had a technician run these prints for us through their AFIS—the Automated Fingerprint Identification System. The search produced a number of aliases. But one of the names, a William Henry Morse, was linked to a two-year hitch in the army, so they assumed that was his original name. George also made use of Morse's aliases—Lassiter, Reynolds, Taylor, and a few others. George was able to match their credit-card buying habits while the 'aliases' were living in cities where past bilking had occurred."

All the players leaned in to listen. Rosa, who already had her hand on the doorknob, returned to the table. Darby gripped her cane with two hands, and Lori relocked the brakes on her wheelchair. Betsy turned her chair around and straddled it with her paisley-patterned slacks.

"Go on, don't stop now," urged Lori.

Darby's cheeks flushed with her sense of importance. "In building this profile, George established a geographic movement pattern, repeated purchasing habits, and a unique living style belonging to one man: William Henry Morse. Several of his activities took place in the same small town in Indiana, with one exception. He never rented a hotel or motel room there, so George assumed it was his home base. He—"

"What town was that?" interrupted Betsy.

"Sorry, I can't remember," Darby said. "It was someplace I'm not familiar with and, at my age, I'm grateful for anything I can remember."

"I know just what you mean," said Lori, as she took a polishing cloth to her lenses and replaced the stylish horn-rims on the end of her nose, so she could look over the top.

"Get on with it, girl," droned Lori. "I want to get to bed before the evil little goblins get to me."

"Okay, okay," Darby responded. "Anyway, when George discovered Morse's home base, one of the first things he checked were the banks. Where did the crook do his banking? Once he had that information, George obtained the account balance—close to two-and-a-half million bucks it was!"

"Oh my God! Hey, wait a minute," said Betsy. "How did George get around all those bank privacy laws?"

"Let's put it this way," said Darby. "There are ways and there are ways and some of them are questionable. That's why anything we discuss here can't leave this room. Is that understood?" One by one, she stared down the players until she obtained a nodding consent from each of them.

"George, the PI, probably hacked into the bank's software to get that balance," offered Rosa. When the rest of the players stared at her in surprise, Rosa replied, "I saw it on *Law and Disorder* just last week."

"We don't know how he accomplished this," Darby reiterated. "He may have done it legally. We just don't know. But this brings us to another issue. George is now awaiting instructions from us before he can do anything more. He can turn over all he has learned now to the FBI and wait for a criminal trial to bring Morse to justice."

"What about all the money we lost to Lassiter?" asked Rosa. "I'd like to recover at least some of my losses."

"That would have to come in a civil class-action trial afterward," declared Betsy.

"And then the damn lawyers would take a big chunk, at least a third, of anything recovered," griped Ralph.

"Yeah!" agreed Darby.

"True," said Rosa. "And wouldn't this all take months and maybe even years?"

Butch piped in. "Who wants to wait that long for money that's rightfully ours now? It's not even earning bank interest for us."

"The lawyers have to make a living, too, you know," defended Betsy. "They're the ones taking the risk when they accept a contingency case. If nothing is recovered, they get nada. And there are court costs as well. Besides, they're the ones who do battle for what is rightly owed."

In a placating tone, Darby said, "Friends, those are all good points. But you might be interested to hear there is a second offer from George. He wants to know—if there were a way to bypass the lawyers and considerably shorten the wait, would we, as a group, be interested?"

"Would this so-called way be legal?" asked Betsy.

"I don't know," said Darby. "I guess there's always some risk."

"Not like drawing to fill an inside straight, I hope," said Butch.

"By the way, what would George get out of this?" asked Lori. "How would he be paid?"

Darby relayed what she'd learned. "George has generously agreed to work for fifteen percent of the recovery amount, plus expenses, no matter how this thing turns out. Why? His mother is one of the victims!"

A shocked silence fell over the group.

Darby's pale green eyes brightened. "Know what? That bit of news makes me trust him. He has a personal stake in helping his mother. So, ladies and gentlemen, it is best that none of us know any of the details." She took a deep breath. "Pay attention, everyone. This is how it would work. The recovered money, less George's fees and expenses, will appear in a dummy escrow account in some remote bank. According to the documented original losses, it would be equitably distributed to all the bilked seniors by an agent as though it were nontaxable insurance from a deceased George Filmore. Only there would be no official record of this. And, of course, in case you hadn't already guessed, that is not our PI's real name."

"Does this mean that bastard, Lassiter or Morse or whatever his name is, gets off scot free?" asked Ralph.

"Not at all. The evidence would be turned over to the FBI anyway," replied Darby.

"How do we go about making this choice?" asked Lori.

Betsy chimed in. "Why don't we do a blind vote? Folded pieces of paper with either a "Yes" or a "No" on them. "Yes" means we agree to let George go ahead. "No" means we disagree. That way we'll never know which option won until this thing plays out. Even then, we won't know who voted which way. Then none of us can be blamed for the way it turns out."

"Whoever counts the ballots will know," said Butch.

"That's true," said Darby. "Why not let George count the ballots? We can put them in a sealed envelope and give it to him with an explanation."

All six eager elderly heads nodded their agreement.

Lori tore six pages out of the back of her treasurer's notebook and distributed them to her fellow players. She rolled her wheelchair over to the desk and took out a Number Ten envelope from the top drawer. She marked her own ballot and passed the pen. Ten minutes later, she collected all the other marked and folded ballots, stuffed them in the envelope, and sealed it before handing it over to Darby to deliver to George.

All six members of the Seniors' Investment Club returned to their rooms that night feeling edgy. Did they do the right thing?

* * * *

Five months passed. The criminal trial against William Henry Morse began. There were so many victims that none of the six players from Bayside Retirement Residence were called to testify. The evidence was overwhelming and Morse was sentenced to fifteen-to-twenty years for his multiple counts of fraud and confidence schemes.

Rumor had it that the money was still in his hidden account. Had Morse volunteered to hand over this money as restitution, his sentence would have been considerably lighter. He claimed to the court that he'd gambled away all of the claimants' money—there was nothing left. Accepting the longer sentence was his proof of that. Thus, without assets, a civil trial would become unproductive.

* * * *

A few days after the end of the criminal trial, P.I. George Filmore discovered that Morse had once again lied. He had not gambled away any of his two-and-a-half million dollars.

The following day, surprise, surprise! All the hidden money disappeared from Morse's account—too late to change his sentence. Any appeal would have to be based on guilt and not on money that no longer existed. It seemed that Morse had drawn to fill the inside straight and lost. What he didn't know, and would never find out, was that all the money he had stolen had been rapidly transferred and distributed to a series of overseas accounts, making it virtually impossible to trace.

A few months later, insurance checks began arriving in all the victims' mailboxes. Only then did our six players begin to understand how their votes went. Supposedly, everyone's losses had been insured by a company called Fairmont Fidelity—and therefore declared an untaxable gain.

* * **

During their next weekly meeting, the six investment club members serenely studied their hands as Butch dealt the cards. They had been discreet, never discussing their votes or the remarkable outcome.

But Rosa insisted on voicing her opinion. "I still think George hacked into Morse's secret account."

"I do not want to know," Darby replied. "But thank you, George, whoever you are."

Forlorn at Fourteen

No matter what Halley Manning did or said, everyone knew she was out of control. Her intentions were mostly good, but she was plagued by a compulsive speech disorder. No matter how hard she tried to be pleasant, she always blurted out inappropriate comments that somehow came across as strokes of meanness. Even her most benign thoughts came out wrong. The fourteen-year-old ninth-grader had no control over them. Poor Halley. This perceived personality flaw left her with no friends at all. Old acquaintances were guarded, and new ones were seldom burned twice. She faced a lonely and unhappy existence.

From afar, Halley looked like an appealing teenager. Her strawberry-blonde hair fell in soft waves over her shoulders. She had hazel eyes that missed nothing, along with smooth pink cheeks, a less than prominent nose, and baby lips. But her charming appearance could not overcome her hapless behavior and inner anguish.

Her parents had attacked her personality problem intelligently. They sent her to medical experts. But the sessions with the psychologist and then the psychiatrist merely served to confuse and agitate her more. After shelling out huge fees for those sessions without any improvement in her behavior, her parents were at their wits' end. In complete frustration, they thought perhaps scolding and punishments would change her compulsive nasty utterances, but such tactics did no good at all. Still, Halley was their daughter. Happy childhood memories from acceptable past behavior balanced all their distress. After all, they loved her no matter what.

Today, nothing had changed. She had insulted her teacher and was sent to the principal's office. Mrs. Manning was called. After school, her mother met her at the front door and shouted, "Go to your room."

Halley plopped down on the guest twin bed in her room with her head in her hands. *It wasn't always this way,* she assured herself. *I once had real friends. What happened to them? When did this all start? Why am I always banished to my room for things I've said or done when they're not my fault? What did I say this time that made my English teacher mad?*

Halley looked up at the two shelves above her own bed—two rows of American Gorgeous dolls of every ethnic depiction. Eighteen male and female dolls dressed for every occasion and every career imaginable—all with diverse, stone-faced expressions.

A rare smile grew on her lips. She rationalized. *The dolls are my friends now. I don't need anyone else.* She reached up and selected Trixie from its high perch and snatched it to her breast—quickly, as though the doll might escape from her grasp. Hugging the doll tightly and swinging it to and fro in her arms, she cried aloud, "I love you, Trixie! You're my best friend forever, my BFF." Halley pranced around the room, mumbling all sorts of endearments to the hunk of porcelain and cloth in her arms. Ten minutes later, she came to a halt in the middle of the room and abruptly held Trixie straight out in front of her.

"Why don't you love me back like other people love their friends?"

When Trixie didn't respond, Halley threw the doll down on the guest bed and slumped next to it, succumbing to another fit of depression. "It isn't fair," she cried. "Why me? I must be cursed."

Halley looked up again at the rows of dolls. She reflected on how she had behaved to pressure her parents to buy each doll.

She had cunningly thrown a mild tantrum for the first one and had improved her tantrum skills for each must-have doll thereafter. But when she set her sights on the Bette Norstrum doll, Mr. and Mrs. Manning told her, "No. We are not paying $300 for a doll!" Still, Halley had persisted. "Please please please!" turned into a super-size tantrum, and *that* behavior resulted in an even sterner "No!" All her screaming failed.

Her parents wouldn't budge, even though she explained how amazing the doll was. Supposedly a clone of rock star Bette Norstrum, it sang in three languages. Even more astounding, when you turned a key in its back, it moved about in circles, thumping a beat just as if it were on stage.

Today, Halley gazed down at the picture of the doll in the catalogue and read the description over and over again. She just had to have this Bette Norstrum doll. *I would do anything, give anything to have it,* she intoned in her mind. *Try me and see.* Just then she heard what sounded like a reverberating gong. It was loud and it lasted for several seconds as it faded. "But what does the gong mean?" she asked herself aloud. She shrugged her shoulders and closed the catalogue.

Two days later, the prized doll arrived on her bed without explanation. Overjoyed, Halley stood Bette up, leaned it against the wall next to her desk, and studied the coveted doll. *Wow, it looks just like the real Bette Norstrum.*

The Bette doll was two feet tall with a sweeping head of black hair that fell seductively over one eye, leaving the other eye of blue glass looking especially intense. Bette wore a hot-pink tank top, matching skin-tight shorts, and thigh-high black boots with stiletto heels. The doll stood, legs apart, holding her guitar in a performance stance.

For several days Halley didn't question her good fortune, nor did her parents ever offer an explanation. But the young girl stewed inside. This ultimate gift scared her. *Had my parents relented because they just couldn't endure any more of my obnoxious behavior? Or,* she wondered, *did I really make a pact with the devil when I said I'd give*

anything to have the Bette Norstrum doll? Maybe I really am cursed.
The evil thought stuck in her mind like a bitter taste you can't seem
to be rid of. Even the words *evil* and *cursed* struck a strange tone—
and it wasn't inside her head. It was that same haunting gong again,
reverberating, then dampening to an eerie silence. *Was it trying to tell
me something?*

Days passed and Halley continued to brood. *Give anything?
That had to be the moment when everything changed—when my par-
ents relented. Oh my God! Did I trade away whatever benign behavior
I had left in me for a Bette Norstrum doll?*

Out of nowhere, without warning, she heard the gong for a
third time, striking louder and longer than before, as though answering her question. It had been silent for days. She gasped. *"Oh no! I
did make a deal with the devil. I'm only fourteen. How could I do that?
More important, how can I undo it?"*

Halley ran her fingers frantically through her thick blonde
tresses. Her eyes glowed with increased intensity as they settled on
Bette. She asked herself: *How can my most prized doll be the source of
my misery?* She reached toward the doll several times, but withdrew
her unwilling arms each time. Then, in one fell swoop, she snatched
it from its place against the wall, and threw it on the hardwood floor.
Halley grew frantic. She tried stomping on Bette's head, but her
sneakers proved too soft to do any damage. Next, she ripped clumps
of the thick, glossy hair from the doll's porcelain head and shredded
them with her sewing scissors. Then, battering the porcelain face
with a wooden shoe tree, she eventually made short work of Bette's
head. The body, the guitar, the shiny boots—all found their way into
her tall wastebasket.

Halley sat down on her bed and shivered at the realization of
what she had done. And she'd made so much noise! How come her
parents hadn't heard her? Exhausted, but feeling quite righteous, she
said aloud, "I'm free at last! Or am I?" She was determined to prove
it to herself.

At seven the next morning, Mom called to her upstairs. "Dad
and I have to leave for work early today. Sorry, dear. Breakfast things

are on the table."

Rushing downstairs to the kitchen, she gobbled up a blueberry muffin and washed it down with a glass of milk. Without her mom and dad present, she could neither test nor profess her newfound freedom. She was about to leave everything on the table, her usual lazy self, when she remembered her resolution of the night before: to be a nicer person. Before leaving for school, she washed her dish and glass and put away the leftover muffins.

Unfortunately, none of the kids at school sensed her new, better self. Two slights and a direct insult later, Halley realized that nothing had changed. Deep down, she knew her outbursts were her own fault. She had been just as annoying, just as bombastic, and just as hurtful as before. *Oh, I'm good at that, all right.*

Walking home from school, Halley racked her brain for answers. *Did I destroy my beautiful Bette for no good reason? Or was my great sacrifice simply not enough?* As she walked through the front door and started up the stairs, the memory of the reverberating gong resounded in her head. *What does the gong mean? Am I still obligated to the devil? What will it take to make me as kind and considerate as I was before I started teeing everyone off?*

That evening, after hurting her parents' feelings with several more unseemly outbursts, Halley found herself in bedroom confinement once more. *What will it take for me to change?* The question kept running through her mind until she looked up at the shelves. Suddenly, she heard another guiding gong tone. *I'm on the right track. The devil wants full measure to be rid of him.*

The doll massacre began. One by one, she lifted each of her remaining seventeen dolls and dealt them the same fate as Bette Norstrum's. Gasping for breath, she cleaned up her mess and felt a chilling rush, a shiver throughout her young body. Something was happening. "Is my sacrifice sufficient?" she asked herself aloud.

"What sacrifice is that, dear?" asked her mother, standing in the open doorway to her room.

Still trembling, Halley plopped down on her bed, arms across her chest, as if protecting herself. "I got rid of all my dolls so I can be a decent, kind, and considerate person again," she replied.

Her mother eyed the large pile of debris that had once been her daughter's prized possessions. "I know what those dolls meant to you. Why was it necessary to destroy them all? I fail to see the connection between the dolls and your behavior. What's going on?"

"I made a pact with the devil to get Bette Norstrum," Halley explained. "I just finished making amends to break that pact. But it cost me all of my precious dolls to do that."

"That's just nonsense," said her mother. "How could you know how to communicate with the devil? How is that even possible? What do you think you are, an exorcist?" She meant it as a joke, but Halley didn't laugh.

"Mom, in the beginning, I think I just wished for Bette Norstrum so very hard, too hard, and the devil heard me. I said I would give *anything* to have her, but I didn't know what I was giving up at the time. It turned out to be my decency, my attitude toward others. My behavior got even worse than before. I'm so sorry." She threw her arms around her mother and hugged her tightly for the first time in almost two years.

Her startled mother hugged back and asked, "Why didn't you come to Daddy or me about this?"

"I didn't know until last night. I really love you, Mom—Daddy too, and I'm sorry for all the trouble I caused."

"Last night? What happened last night?"

Halley's arms dropped to her sides and she stepped back to look her mother in the eye. "I heard this tone. It kinda helped me make the right decision to get rid of the dolls."

"Tone? what kind of tone?"

"It sounded like someone hitting one of those big scary gongs, and it lingered for a while. Whenever I questioned anything or hesitated over one choice or another, the gong always seemed to prefer one answer over the other. I know it was all in my head, but it worked, didn't it?"

"Apparently so, dear," her mother replied. "It certainly was all in your head, All of it. But whatever the reason, I'm glad to have you back. Maybe it adds credence to the old cliché 'Careful what you wish for, it may come true.'"

Halley's mother smiled with secret thoughts she would never reveal to her daughter. *I'd better not tell her that I was responsible for the gong's reverberating sound. My striking the knickknack Chinese gong in the living room must have coincided with her reasoning. I struck the gong accidentally while dusting, and I listened until the resonance dissipated. I was so pleased with the tone that I struck it several more times. If the gong brought about our daughter's better behavior, so be it. But one thing's for sure. We will never buy Halley another doll.*

Mom and Dad were thrilled to have their darling daughter back—good-natured, helpful with household chores, and getting along at school with her teachers and classmates.

A Woolly Place in Time

What the devil is happening? Just being playful, I sit down in-side Levi Levin's time machine, and our *meshugge* friend Ar-nie, a real nut, leans in and pushes the SEND button! The Levins' living room goes poof! Gone are sofa, recliner, drapes, and coffee table. So where in time and space do I wind up? Here. But where in heaven's name is Here?

All I can see for miles in any direction is sand and rocks and creepy insects. The sun is beating down with unabashed glee. With-out a hat, I feel like a sizzling *latke* in a frying pan, a potato pancake. Whew! I'm getting out of this sweater. A lot of good cashmere with silver sparkles is doing me here in the wilds. But I'm not abandon-ing it. Just a week ago I spent sixty dollars on it. I'm tying the arms around my waist for now. And I swear I'll suffocate with this paisley scarf around my neck. I'm tying it around my forehead and undo-ing the pearl buttons at the top of my blue dress. Ah, at least I can breathe a little better. Now all I need is a big dose of moxie.

But what's a nice Jewish girl like me, Ida Mossberg, supposed to do? Where can I find shelter from this punishing sun? Way off, I see what looks like tall grasses and mountains. I start trudging that way.

I've been dragging myself along for two hours, and those

mountains still don't look any closer. But I do see a speck ahead of me that seems to be getting larger. Hey, now it's separating into two figures, leaping and running straight toward me through the savannah grass. Thank heaven, I've been discovered! My rescuers are on the way. Maybe they'll lead me out of this godforsaken wasteland.

As the distance closes, I make out a burly man and boy. They appear to be a little taller than my five-foot-five. Closer still, I see they're wearing animal skins, yet not from any animal I recognize. I wonder if there's such a thing as a *Homo sapiens* fashion guide. Wowee—I'm remembering my eighth-grade social studies class. Maybe I'm in the tail end of the Pleistocene Epoch. And maybe those animal skins came from the woolly mammoth, the elephant-sized beasts with shaggy brown fur and huge curved tusks.

Whoa! The man and boy are carrying weapons. Each one has a wooden spear and a club. They must be Cro-Magnons, hunters. *That's* not good. Just my luck. Why couldn't they be Neanderthals—at least *they're* farmers. The man's eyes stare wildly out from a grizzled face as his hairy arm swings the big fat club in a wide circle. I've never been so terrified—right down to my damp Victoria's Secret panties. With a wild scream, the man leaps at me. I hear a loud thud. Then nothing at all.

I wake up in another place. The whole right side of my head throbs, and my sight is fuzzy. Now I remember. The bastard used his wretched club on me. I'm lying on my left hip in front of a fire. Everything else is dark. We're in a cave! What did I expect, a three-bedroom condo?

My wrists and ankles are tied tight with some kind of vine. These guys are scaring me. I bet they're cannibals. Oh, yeah. I'm going to be roasted alive on a spit. All that's missing is the barbeque basting sauce. I struggle to a sitting position and note three humans glaring at me from the other side of the fire: the man, the boy, and a female. They're all squarely built and muscular. Their faces have wide foreheads and high, thick cheekbones. The man who clubbed my head squats just opposite me. I'll call him Og. He watches me sit up, wiggling helplessly trying to get free, and starts to jabber at me in a tongue I can't begin to understand. His tone turns to frustration, then anger when I fail to respond. The boy looks like he might be a teenager, with fuzzy jaws begging to be shaved. I'll call him Om. He interjects his opinion, and Og swats him with the back of a heavy hand, knocking him over. The entertainment ain't all that bad, but it's tough not having a program.

Okay, enough sarcasm. What do these beings want with me? The nape of my neck tingles despite the heat of the fire. Goosebumps cover my bare arms. Fear crawls up my spine, or is it a deadly spider? The silent, expressionless female sits cross-legged next to Om. I'll call her Er. She has less facial hair than her mate; a leathery map of wrinkles is printed there instead. Her lava-black locks look like an explosion of frizz. Her hairdresser must be on vacation. In her thick hands, she steadies a huge chunk of meat skewered onto a pointed bare branch over the fire. A woolly mammoth drumstick? Clearly, I'm invited to dinner, but I'm still not sure in what capacity. Does it mean I get at least a one meal's reprieve before they roast me, too?

My eyes are becoming more accustomed to the light now, so I take in my surroundings. A few yards away, I see my paisley scarf and white sweater actually folded on the dirt floor, still surprisingly clean. The cave is large and deep, made of coarse rock walls and a stone ceiling, possibly high enough that I could stand up. That is, if they ever unbind me and allow me to stand. In the flickering firelight I can't seem to locate an entrance. Either the opening is hidden around a bend, or it's simply nighttime beyond.

Suddenly, in the shadows I notice a fourth figure: a less hairy young male with fairer skin and a somewhat clipped black beard. He sits by himself a few feet away. I'll call him El. He's staring back at me with fierce dark eyes. Oh-oh, that look! Is El finding me sexually attractive or is he merely working up his digestive juices to devour me? Either way, I want out! I'm only eighteen. I don't belong here. I want to be back in Levi Levin's living room making jokes about his stupid time machine. Or better still, back in my family's cozy breakfast nook, where we're all eating toasted bagels smeared with lots of cream cheese and topped with a slice of lox. And I want my mommy!

The fire crackles and sizzles. Er keeps a firm grip on the meat over the fire as it turns dark, then almost burnt. Og bellows a command. He grabs the skewer from Er, holds it still, and sits motionless for a minute or two, his biceps bulging from the drumstick's weight. And then, with a remarkably civilized gesture, he blows a few whiffs of breath to cool it. With brown, mottled teeth, a powerful chomp of his jaw, and a violent jerk of his neck, Og shears away a whole strip off the drumstick. He shreds and chews while the others watch. My dentist would be having a field day here. Og would make a great "Before" in a teeth-whitener ad. He finally rubs his stomach and passes the meat skewer to the boy. With his teeth, Om pulls the meat from the stick, holding on with both hands, imitating his father, but with less violence. When he's done, he rubs his stomach, wipes his mouth with the back of his arm, and passes the skewer to his mother.

Without waiting for Er to finish eating, father and son get to their feet and turn to leave the fireside. I make a little disturbance, a noticeable cough, to attract Og's attention. He turns back, looks down at me, and smirks. I put on my most pleading look and hold out my hands in their bonds for him to see. This he understands quite well, but chooses to ignore my plight anyway. For a second there is even a smile of superiority on his lips. He's got plans for me, but for what? The suspense is killing me. I hope not literally.

The hairy father and son turn away once more and lumber toward a heap of furs along the far wall. Both walk with a serious hunch in their backs. I'm guessing it's normal posture for them, like an old man with osteoporosis—even for young Om, who can be no older than sixteen. Er finishes her meal, as if every bite is painful. She sets the giant drumstick, still with meat on it, down on a rock, and joins her husband and son along the far wall. Hey, everyone, what about me? Don't I count? I'm starving!

El, seeing the empty places around the fire, approaches and slides into the place left by Er. Without looking up once, he grabs the drumstick and chomps, tears, chews, and swallows, until satisfied. After he finishes, he turns his gaze toward me. He's grinning broadly now, with healthy yet stained teeth. The meat juices are still dripping down both cheeks to his chin—oddly, the juices shine in the firelight. El draws the back of his hand across his face in one grand wipe, and I see that his facial features are not unattractive.

What now? The man can't be hungry after all that.

There's still some meat left. El holds it up as if offering me sloppy fifths on this communal delicacy. Thank you, woolly mammoth! But why is he feeding me? To fatten me up for tomorrow's lunch? Oh, hell, I haven't eaten all day, and it doesn't look like I'll be getting any better offers to dine out. I nod. He stands and works his way around the fire toward me. I see by the shadows that he's sturdy and well-proportioned. He's also clothed in the shaggy animal skins. But there the similarities with the cave family end. El is taller and stands erect.

Ugh! As he steps closer, I get a powerful whiff of the guy. He hasn't bathed for about six months. Maybe longer. He stinks! But who cares? I'm hungry! I hold out my bound hands again, hoping he takes pity on me, but no, El merely places what's left of the meat in my grip. Okay, I'll survive. He sits beside me, watching my every move while I tackle the meat. A knife, fork, dinner plate, and free hands would do wonders here, but I do the best I can and manage to eat my fill. I can't wait to get back home and tell Mom what I had for dinner. Her first reaction will be, "Is woolly mammoth Kosher?"

The drumstick is now a bare bone about a yard long. El stands up, walks over to a wall, and stores it inside a rectangular rock ledge, a clever cubby hole. Ambling back, he sits down and slides closer to me until our shoulders are touching. So close I sense his foul breath. I conquer my repulsion and show him my bound wrists. He ignores me and, instead, pulls my head gently against his mostly hairless chest. In a strangely caressing way, he toys with my tangled hair, entwining the long, thick strands around his slender fingers. Then he pats the smoothness of my cheeks and strokes my neck. I'm worried, but decide it's best not to resist. Besides, I could use a friend right now.

I look up at his face and I can tell he finds my smooth skin pleasing. I get the message—I know where this is going. My body is sensing it, too. Even my sense of smell is being neutralized. But once more I hold up my sore wrists. El reaches under his animal skin and retrieves a sharp stone blade. I figure this is it. He's ready for dessert. My time has come to an end.

Trembling, I start to pull away. El waves the blade toward my neck, but changes direction and, with one swipe, cuts and unwraps my bindings. I flex my hands and arms. Happily, he doesn't stop there. He frees my ankles as well. I try to stand up so I can stretch my achy muscles. He helps me to my feet and tugs me toward the nearest wall. I hesitate and he flashes his blade once more. *Oy-oy*. I'm getting mixed messages here. I surrender and follow him.

I don't believe it. Animal furs, laid out on the ground, are the length and width of twin-sized beds! I happily collapse and curl up to sleep, arms and legs free.

The next morning, I wake up to find Og standing over me with his club. I can only assume he knows I'm no longer tied up. I can't tell if he's angry or not. He starts to raise his club from his side. Both my hands fly up to cover my head, especially where that knot on top is still smarting from yesterday's blow. But I'm not his target after all. Og leans over and, with his club, raps the sleeping El hard on the rump. El's eyes pop open and he jerks up to a sitting position. Og is babbling. But his mood changes. He's now beaming from ear to ear, with his huge crooked, brown teeth. What gives? Maybe he's celebrating El's conquest. Does he think El is also his son? My body freezes, my breathing gets shallow as I wait and watch.

Actually, nothing happens. Perhaps I even have the dad's approval. I figure that marriage rites haven't been invented yet, so as far as Og is concerned, El and I are mates—like it or not. Am I destined to have a caveman father-in-law? What's my probable inheritance here? My dowry? Og starts to walk away.

Revealing all my anxiety and distress, I blurt out, "Oh, crap! I miss my darling golden retriever. My Toyota Corolla. Cupcakes with butter-cream frosting. Passover with *matzoh*. And I want to brush my teeth!"

I see El shushing me with a forefinger vertical on his lips. Hey! That gesture isn't from this godforsaken time period. Something's fishy here. Then, to my great surprise and in perfect English, El says, "I'll explain as soon as Og is out of earshot."

Minutes later, El sits me down on a flat rock, looks me straight in the eye, and reveals the truth. "I'm also the victim of a time machine prank. I've been here for a bunch of years with no way out. But it's my own fault. My real name is Maury Levin. I'm Levi Levin's older brother, the one who went missing so many years ago. I was an engineer, an inventor, and I even had a few patents to my name. My last invention was the time machine. When I tested it, I was exhilarated! I thought I'd get rich and famous. But I had made one huge, horrible mistake. I didn't invent a way to get back to the Twenty-Second Century."

Maury stops talking and waits for his words to sink in, anxiously watching my face for a reaction.

I'm too stunned to reply. My heart drops to my toes. If *he's* trapped, so am I. Oh my God! I want my life back! I was a budding sculptor. Will I ever be able to create art again? I have noticed an array of tools and weapons lined up against one wall—even a graceful figurine there that one of them had carved. I remember something else from my eighth-grade social studies class: Cro-Magnons had those kinds of skills. Maybe the family will let me use some of the tools for my art.

It takes me ten minutes to calm down. At least that's what my Timex watch says. When it needs a new battery, what will I use? A sundial? What a joke. I'm quite sure it hasn't been invented yet.

I try to console myself. Maybe I shouldn't complain. Life might be a good deal simpler here without tough bosses, appliances that break down, credit card balances, and social biases.

Resigned to my fate, I reach out for Maury's hand. During the next few weeks, we become great friends. He's so much the gentleman that soon I have to become the aggressor. We're now mates and we don't need a stone *katuba* (marriage certificate) to prove it. The prospects of our returning to the Twenty-Second Century are nil. How can we initiate such a transfer through Time from this end? How can the time machine ever find us when we don't even know where we are? Or what year we're in. I've noticed a small carved section on one wall that looks like some kind of calendar, but it's surely indecipherable to me.

As the months go by, I resign myself to this life. I'm learning the caveman language and Maury is helping me. By the way, I'm pregnant with our first child. Young Om is teaching us to hunt, and that is quite exciting. In return, Maury and I teach Og and Er and Om what little we know about planting and harvesting.

Tomorrow Maury and I are going cave hunting. We agreed that a two-grotto cave, with a built-in hearth and smooth rock dinette set, will suit us perfectly. If we can find a nearby stream or brook, it will satisfy our only utility requirement.

But will we be required to get a mortgage? I chuckle. The concept hasn't been invented yet. Which is lucky. What would I put down on the application for my age? Minus ten thousand and twenty-four?

The Old Gold Watch

Jonathan Quincy Dembleford winced from arthritis as he reached with trembling fingers into the waistband pocket of his trousers to retrieve his watch. He flipped open the eighteen-karat gold cover and squinted until he made out the time of day. *Earlier than I thought.* He raised the antique timepiece to his ear to be sure it was still working. Weakly, *tick, tick, tick. I guess I have a little time left. I wonder where they are. They're supposed to be here by now.*

He didn't need to see the photo of the lovely but stern-looking young woman set into the inside cover of the watch. But tired eyes landed there anyway. *My darling Florence wasn't stern at all. She just posed that way—everyone did in those days.* He'd outlived his wife of sixty-three years by fifteen years, and his only son, Jasper, by eight years. He pressed the cover closed and ran his thumb across its leafy-patterned gold surface. Turning the watch over to the smooth gold side, he ran his thumb over the engraved letters. Consoling himself, he reflected. *So, I'm an old fart of ninety-seven. That doesn't mean I've forgotten the words I've carried in my pocket most of my life.* He repeated them aloud. **"Whoever Winds Me Faithfully Shall Live a Full Life."**

Jonathan's brain and memory still chugged along on all cylinders like a prized antique car. It was his once strong body that had deserted him—and so had the relatives and friends he grew up with. He had outlived all his contemporaries. At this moment he had little reason, and even less finger strength, to wind the notched gold crown, the knob used for setting or adjusting the time. He had no idea just how many ticks were left—or how many breaths were left for him to take. But he knew there weren't many. Stretching out his gnarled left hand with great effort, he laid the watch down on the night table and fumed aloud, "Where is my family?"

Despite his weakened body, his thoughts still vibrated with the vigor of a patriarch. His long face and sharp cheekbones now drooped into a jowled chin, but his deep blue eyes still challenged anyone who confronted him. He prided himself on the thick swath of white hair that fell across his high forehead. *No balding for me,* he always noted with satisfaction in front of his bathroom mirror.

With his head propped on a pillow, Jonathan lay on the coverlet of his king-size bed in his Sunday best: a starched white shirt, silk tie, charcoal-gray three-piece suit—and even his polished black wing-tip shoes. He had planned his outfit with great care and had left instructions to be buried in it. *No way am I going to lie here in bed in a pathetic flannel nightshirt like some senile old fool.*

He expected the Grim Reaper, but felt himself very much in control. First, he needed to meet with the few remaining members of the Dembleford clan. He had something precious to pass along to Jason, his favorite grandson. There was only one problem: Jason had a twin brother, Jerome, and there was only one gold watch to hand down. The grandfather had brooded for months. *Will my watch become a bone of contention between the twins?* At twenty-two years old, they couldn't be any closer. He didn't want to destroy, or even disturb, the loving camaraderie that had existed between them since their births. Their attractive mother died in an auto accident when the twins were twelve, so even she wouldn't be there to referee any rift that might grow out of this bequest of the watch. The old man had been careful how he handled the whole inheritance thing. The twins would inherit, in equal measure, their grandfather's respectable investment portfolio. But what to do about the gift of the watch?

Jonathan had mulled over one possible solution: to replicate the watch down to its most intricate details and even the marks of its true age. Then, swapping the two enough times so that no one, including himself, would know which watch was the original, he could award his grandsons seemingly identical gifts. Length of life for the two grandsons would thus be left to Lady Luck. But no jeweler he approached had either the time or inclination to take on the project. Unfortunately, Jonathan did have a favorite grandson, and with good reason. Although Jerome was always polite, he was also habitually aloof. Jason, on the other hand, had a more tender and emotional temperament, and loved spending time with his grandfather. Despite the decades between them, they played chess and gin rummy (but only for pennies) and watched television together, Their favorite shows: *The West Wing* and *Downton Abbey*. They laughed themselves silly over Carol Burnett's outrageous skits. Jason read to him—his own favorite novels, including *Treasure Island* and *The Three Musketeers*.

But Jonathan brooded. If he gave the precious watch to Jason, what would he give his twin brother instead? He decided that Jerome would get the family dwelling—a sprawling, but aging farmhouse of stone and clapboard, with many bedrooms that needed freshening, and impulsively added wings. The house was slightly eccentric but full of charm, set on twenty acres of uncultivated meadow and trees.

* * * *

Six months earlier, Jonathan spent a whole day with his trusted attorney, Samuel Smythe, dictating the terms of his will. Samuel had been the family's legal and financial adviser for fifty years. When he heard Jonathan's wishes, he blinked twice and raised his startled eyebrows.

"It's sensible and fair that the twins will share your investment portfolio. But Jonathan, what's this other half-cocked idea? You're leaving Jerome your thirty-room house on all those beautiful acres—and only giving Jason, your favorite grandson, your old watch? Good grief, my friend! Where's the logic in that?" To the attorney the implications were obvious. The house and property dominated the New Hampshire town where they lived. Jerome would possess both prominence and influence.

Jonathan's dark blue eyes burned with conviction. He had no intention of spelling out his reasoning. He knew he would sound slightly batty, as if his mind had entered a realm of half-witted fantasy. In truth, he deeply and strongly believed that the watch had a mystical attribute: the power to bestow longevity.

* * * *

That Sunday morning, just when he feared that his family wouldn't arrive on time, he heard two car doors slam outside his window. Minutes later, the twins came through the bedroom door to be at his side. At great length he explained the terms of his will—and the powers of the watch. Never before had he imparted his secret to anyone. Then his voice began to fail, lapsing into a whisper so faint the twins could no longer hear him. But he had already given them the reasoning behind his bequests. Jason picked up the watch and pressed it to his right ear. Not even a single tick. The watch had stopped. He bent over his grandfather's chest to listen for a heartbeat. Not even a single beat. The wound-down gold watch could no longer sustain the old man's life.

"Rest in peace, dear Grandpa," said Jason. He bent over, pushed aside the shock of white hair, and kissed the wrinkled forehead.

"Thank you for everything," said Jerome as he reached for his grandfather's hand and brought it to his lips. In truth, he was overwhelmed by his grandfather's generosity, which he felt he hardly deserved. "Hey, Jason, aren't you going to wind the watch like Grandpa said?" he asked.

"Of course," said Jason. He picked up the timepiece and began to wind. "But I'm not sure I believe in its powers of longevity."

When he finished, he lifted the watch to his right ear, anxious to hear if it was working once again. *Tick, tick, tick.* "Yes!"

"Maybe you have to believe in order for its powers to work," said Jerome.

"Maybe," agreed Jason.

The funeral was held two days later, and the will was executed the following month.

* * * *

Thirty-three years later found the twins in a good place. Both investment portfolios had prospered despite several recessions. They both had moved into separate wings in their grandfather's mansion. Jerome was in his third term as mayor of Dembleford Township. Jason was working on his thirteenth mystery novel, having successfully published a dozen before it. Each of the twins had married happily. Jason was blessed with a married daughter and Jerome with a married son, and six grandchildren between them.

The outlook seemed rosy until Jerome came home from a routine doctor visit with a shocking diagnosis. He had pancreatic cancer and only eight months to live. A stoical sort, Jerome kept his imminent demise a secret, even from his family. Then, for the first time in years, he remembered Grandpa's watch. He knew his brother didn't believe in the watch's powers, but kept it wound faithfully nonetheless, in keeping with his devotion to Grandpa Jonathan.

Jerome wasn't so sure about the powers either, but he felt it was worth a try. He revealed his plight to his brother and asked if he might wear and wind the old gold watch for however long he might need it. Good-natured Jason enjoyed robust health, so he agreed to lend the watch to his twin. An amazing thing happened. Jerome went into remission and within two months was free of all symptoms.

Another six years of good health and prosperity passed before Jason was hospitalized with a severe heart attack. He survived bypass surgery, but soon learned that the cardiologists had missed a horrific problem. Jason was diagnosed with an enlarged heart. He had only three months to live. He desperately wanted Grandpa's watch back. But how could he ask his brother to surrender it? The twins both believed its powers provided the sustaining element of Jerome's life.

Jerome swore he owed his miraculous remission and cure to the watch. But when he learned the terrible news about Jason, he offered to give the old gold watch back to its rightful owner. Jason reluctantly accepted the offer. And, would you believe it? The baffled,

119

but thrilled doctors got his enlarged heart under control. As he began to feel better daily, he became more of a believer in the power of the watch.

One day, while sitting in the doctor's office awaiting a check-up, Jason grew irritated. It was an hour past his scheduled appointment time. Fidgeting in the wooden chair in the waiting room, he kept checking his watch. For no particular reason, he turned it over on its expansion band and studied the inscription on the smooth side: "Whoever Winds Me Faithfully Shall Live a Full Life." He had not looked at the inscription for decades, but now, a full believer, Jason suddenly had a great thought. The word "whoever" doesn't necessarily limit the winder to one person. What if Jerome and I share the wearing and the winding? Won't we both get the most out of life?

The old gold watch took eight turns of the notched crown to fully wind it for a fifty-hour run. So, Jason and Jerome each took four turns of the gold crown every other day. The result? They both lived decades longer in good health and died at age ninety-five within seconds of each other.

But not before successfully solving the same knotty problem that their grandfather, Jonathan Quincy Dembleford, had faced. The old gold watch would be left to one of the grandchildren. But from then on, the winding of the stem had to be shared, equally and responsibly, among all the grandchildren.

Our Own Menehune Legends

A millennium ago there existed in Hawai'i a race of people called the Menehune, small in stature as well as industrious in nature. How do we know about them? Fishponds and walls constructed a thousand years ago, together with a number of anthropological relics, skeletal remains, and an oral history bolster the existence of these remarkable little people.

According to the legends, the Menehune ranged in size from six inches to two feet. Wave-shaped hats and mere loincloths, dye-colored to reflect their hierarchy in the tribal community, covered their nakedness. Green-leafed bracelets adorned their ankles. Most Menehune were well-proportioned, muscular, eager to be helpful, and well-suited to all sorts of work.

Sadly, the Menehune all bore the same nametag given to them by uninformed humans: *lola moe halau*, meaning "lazybones." Those intrusive humans who secretly observed them did not understand that these tiny people slept by day and worked by the moon and stars at night. So the Menehune mostly dealt with humans in a fitting way. Outsiders stumbling upon their presence were induced on the spot into a deep sleep and, upon awakening, couldn't recall or be certain of anything they'd seen.

Thus, the Menehune existed in secrecy for more than a thousand years. With only a few exceptions, these tiny people have managed to remain hidden from Hawaiians, Asians, and *haoles* alike by choosing to live in the wild and distant fringes where other beings seldom tread.

Through the years, sages have expanded and embellished this rich lore. As authors, we have been so captivated by these stories, especially *The Three Menehune of Ainahou* by Charles Kauluwehi Maxwell Sr., that we have chosen to invent our own four Menehune legends. Our thanks to "Uncle Charley" for his inspiration. We created these legends with love and respect for Hawaiian lore.

—*Rosemary and Larry Mild*

The Legend of Makaio

On most sunny afternoons Makaio slept somewhere out of sight, clad only in his red and gray loincloth. His wiry body, twenty-two inches long, curled to fit precisely into his favorite hidden recess in the rocky cliffs of Kaua'i.

There's a slight bit of mischief hiding in all Menehune. But Makaio had honed his own prank-loving side to an unwelcome degree, garnering complaints from the community elders. They considered his inventive activities a blatant nuisance. For his latest exploit, he had secretly prowled the lavish garden of a rich human family and switched many newly planted bulbs to unlikely spots. Months later, tulips popped up amid carrots and cornstalks. Scallions and huge taro leaves grew amid delicate orchids.

Four Menehune elders, in their white loincloths and feathered headdresses, assembled this very night to pass judgment on Makaio. A rare two-month expulsion from the tribe was their unanimous decision.

Makaio packed his sparse belongings into a cloth sack and hung it on a pole over his shoulder. With a single tear lingering on his shiny bronze cheek, he started down the wooded trail in the dark of night. To where? He didn't care where—he was too upset.

The trail widened to a paved road that opened onto a restful hamlet of Hawaiian bungalows. Not a single resident stirred until the tiny blue dot on the eastern horizon suddenly became the first explosion of dawn. Makaio realized he needed a place to hide until nightfall. He just couldn't betray the Menehune tradition of secrecy or he'd never be readmitted to the tribe.

He took stock of his surroundings and settled on a rain barrel standing next to the front lanai of a nearby dwelling. Half-full of water, the barrel was made of three-foot-high wooden staves held together by iron rings. Using all his strength, Makaio pushed it on its side to empty it. He hopped aside to avoid soaking his slippers, as the water formed a large puddle before draining down the sloping grade. When he was certain the barrel was free of water, he wiggled inside, feet first, his head resting within six inches of the barrel's opening. He fell fast asleep within minutes.

Unknown to Makaio, the bungalow belonged to Auntie Nele, who always slept late to suit her advancing years. When she finally arose that morning, her routine took her outside to the very rain barrel where Makaio was sleeping. She needed to draw water from it for her morning's drinking and washing. Puzzled by the toppled barrel, she shook her head and tried to set it upright. Although she was stronger and healthier than most *wahine* (ladies) her age, it proved to be a harder task than she expected. As she pulled and tugged the barrel upright, wobbling it into its vertical position, a tiny head popped up like a jack-in-the-box. Auntie Nele gasped, jumped backward, and fell flat on her *ōkole*. She screamed so loud that Makaio feared she'd wake the entire hamlet. He shrank back into his hiding place again.

Not hearing another sound for some minutes, Makaio peeked out of the barrel top. His keen eyes darted about and spied the large Hawaiian woman lying awkwardly in the puddle next to the barrel. He hoisted himself out and cautiously approached her. Her eyes were closed, alarming him, for Menehune were committed to doing no harm to others. But then he noticed the floral-patterned mu'umu'u rising and falling on her chest at a regular yet quickened rate and realized the woman had fainted at the sight of him. Feeling responsible, he decided to wake her and see if he could come to her rescue. He ran his fingers through the puddle of clear water and sprinkled drops all over her island-brown face.

Soon Auntie Nele's head shook to one side and then the other in order to avoid more drops. In a few seconds both eyes opened, and her head jerked up, taking in the image of the elfin man standing so close. Frightened, her first impulse was to get away from this strange being. "Who? No, *what* are you?" she shrieked. But then she recognized what she believed to be a Menehune from pictures in the book of Hawaiian legends she kept on the mantle over the fireplace. Before Makaio could answer, Auntie sat upright. Her left hand shot out and her fingers clamped tightly about his right ankle.

"Let me go," he protested. "I didn't mean to frighten you. I just needed a place to hide during daylight."

Auntie kept a tight grip on his ankle as she climbed to her feet. "I'm Auntie Nele. You're a Menehune, aren't you?"

Makaio knew that Menehune are incapable of lying. "Yes, but you're hurting me. Please let me go."

Auntie Nele ignored his plea. Hoisting him over her shoulder like a sack of potatoes, she carried him into the house, and set him down on the kitchen counter, still gripping his ankle firmly. With wrapping cord from a utility drawer beneath the counter, she tied his tiny feet together..

Makaio wiggled and squirmed. "Untie me, please," he begged in his most contrite voice. "I won't run away."

"I'd be a fool to let you go," Auntie said. "I understand that you Menehune have the power to grant us humans wishes. What kind of wishes can you grant me?"

Makaio raised his eyebrows one by one, a charming technique he had mastered for his own amusement. "How do you know I can grant you any wishes at all?"

Auntie placed her large hands on her ample hips. "I read it in my book of legends, so it must be true. Stop stalling and tell me."

"Well, I can't give you wealth or any material things, but I can pledge to do work for you for a time."

"A time? How long is that?" she demanded.

Makaio thought about the length of his tribal expulsion period. "It would be for sixty days. I can't work any longer than that."

"What kind of work can you do for me?"

"I can do all your daily chores and make all sorts of improvements around the house, too. Under three conditions. One, you allow me to sleep in the house during the daytime. Two, you provide me with the same meals you eat. And three, I'll need to do all the work after sundown."

Auntie thought for several moments. At sixty-four, overweight and lazy, even having the daily chores done would be a welcome vacation for her. And his conditions seemed reasonable. "How do I know you won't run off as soon as I untie you?"

"I give you my word. Besides, that book of legends you mentioned will tell you that Menehune don't and, in fact, can't lie."

"Okay, I believe you," said Auntie as she unraveled the cords around Makaio's ankles. "My name is Auntie Nele. What's yours?"

"I am called Makaio. Now, Auntie, you must let me sleep until nightfall, as I cannot be seen working for you," declared the little man as he slipped off the counter to the floor.

Auntie frowned. "But you simply can't sleep in my bed. I only have one bed in the house."

"Don't worry your big head about that," Makaio answered. "I'm used to sleeping in hard places, because I weigh less than eighteen pounds in my altogether. In fact, I see a cozy place right over there." He pointed to the small pantry, where a multicolored, braided rug covered the floor.

"My head is not big." With both hands, she dramatically fluffed up her mop of white hair.

"It is to me."

"Well, that's offensive, so keep your comments to yourself."

Auntie lowered herself into a kitchen chair and watched him pick a spot on the pantry rug, where he curled up. He closed his eyes, then popped one of them open to catch her staring at him. He reached out and pulled the pantry door partly closed. Minutes later, Auntie heard a strange buzzing sound. She peeked around the door and determined that the sound was a Menehune snore. A motherly instinct arose as she saw how peacefully he slept. She took a clean, dry dish towel from a kitchen drawer and covered him up before tiptoeing from the room.

Settling into her recliner, the Hawaiian woman turned to her favorite daily routines: weaving; reading her newspaper; or listening to soaps on the radio. Today she also read snippets from the family book of legends to learn more about Menehune. After all, the little guy would be her guest for the next two months, so she should know a bit about him. When she finished cooking her supper, she left a covered bowl for Makaio. Just after dusk she retired to her bed, because she didn't want to use costly electricity to light the rooms. Yes, she was a stingy woman.

When Auntie Nele awoke the next morning, she sensed something was different, but couldn't quite put her finger on it. She noticed that her bedroom had an unusually tidy look. Then she saw a fresh muʻumuʻu and undergarments laid out on the chair by her bed. Auntie dressed and slowly walked through her bungalow. The living room, dining room, and kitchen were all spotless, even to the point of a shine. Eggs, bacon, toast, and coffee sat on the perfectly set kitchen table. The rest of her laundry looked clean and folded on a chair opposite where she usually sat. At the front door to pick up the daily paper, Auntie saw that the lawn had been mowed and the yard raked of its clippings. Back in the kitchen, she noticed the pantry door remained slightly ajar, so she peeked around it. Makaio was curled up on the rug fast asleep with the same towel draped across his body. She quietly sat down to eat her breakfast. All through that day, Auntie continued to see the benefits of his efforts. She smiled to herself. *I've made an excellent bargain with that little man.*

As the days progressed, Auntie Nele's to-do list grew by leaps and bounds. The house was painted inside and out. The window panes sparkled. A white picket fence appeared around the bungalow's tiny lawn, and several cords of wood had been chopped for the fireplace. Even an extra room had been added. Improvements too numerous to count had been accomplished until she couldn't think of anything more for Makaio to do except for the daily chores. She took full measure of their deal, working him hard, and Makaio complied without complaint.

On the last day of their agreement, Auntie Nele suffered pangs of regret, knowing that he would be moving on. She would have to do her own chores again! She woke him up that morning and asked him, "What would it take for us to extend our agreement for another month or longer?"

Makaio yawned and scowled. "As I told you in the beginning, there's an absolute sixty-day limit on our agreement. I have kept my bargain. I can't work for you any longer. I'm leaving for home tonight after dusk." He rolled on his side and pulled the towel up over his head.

Ignoring her only made the vindictive Auntie Nele angry, so she headed for the counter drawer once more and retrieved the ball of heavy twine. Flipping the dish towel off him, she started to wrap both Makaio's legs together.

"Wait!" he shouted. "What are you doing to me? I've been more than fair with you. I gave you sixty days' worth of honest labor, just as I promised, and now you want to take me captive again?"

"Yeah," Auntie retorted. "I'm too old to be doing chores. I want to keep you around, little fellow."

"But I'm not able to extend or make new promises."

"How come that's not in the legends book?"

Makaio's small voice turned shrill. "That book can't reveal every single thing about us. We're a profound and complicated people. Maybe a new chapter should be added telling about humans and what they're really like. How they don't keep their promises. How they're greedy, and no matter how much we do for them, they always demand more."

Auntie Nele took two more tight turns of twine around his legs.

"Ow! Ow! Ow! That hurts! Ow! It's too tight."

"So!" Auntie challenged. "What else can you do for me?"

Unable to lie and desperate to be free of pain, the pitiful Menehune told her: "I can answer one—and only one—question for you about your personal future."

"You mean you can tell me I'll win the lottery?"

"I can tell you *if* you'll win it, but I can't win it for you."

"If?" she sneered. "That's no good. It's not likely anyway, so *if* is no good."

"I *can* tell you *when* something will happen."

"When?" Auntie repeated. "Like...like...the day I'm gonna die?"

"Is that your question?"

"Maybe." Auntie pursed her thick lips and wrinkled her brow as she thought long and hard about it. Then she asked, "How will I know you're telling me the absolute truth?"

"Remember, a Menehune cannot lie."

"Then, yeah. Tell me when."

"Untie me and let me out the door and I'll give you the day you are going to die. Agreed?"

Auntie slowly unwound the twine. When Makaio jumped free, she opened the front door for him. He nimbly slipped outside and pranced a few steps out of her reach.

Auntie became suspicious. "What about the answer to my question?"

"Your demise will come on October twenty-third," he said, hopping back a few more steps.

"But the twenty-third is less than a month away."

"That's true," he said with a lopsided smile on his tiny lips.

"But what about the year?" she persisted. "I need to know the year."

"There you go again, Auntie, breaking another promise. The year? That's another question. One I am under no obligation to answer."

Makaio took a few more buoyant leaps away and disappeared into the woods beyond the village. He returned to his tribe. For all we know, when his daily work was done, he was still making mischief—but careful how and when, so he'd never have to meet up with a human again.

Makaio had left Auntie with a curse for being so mean to him. That year, and for twenty more afterward, she dreaded the approach of October twenty-third, fearing each one would be her last.

The Legend of Elikai

Elikai was a Menehune, one of the little people of the deep forest. He stood sixteen inches from his sandals to the top of his funny wave-shaped hat. A bit thick in the waist might be a good way to describe him, for when the opportunity arose, he never turned down an extra mouthful. In fact, he was known to create culinary opportunities as his own joyous occupation.

Elikai was a talented baker—cakes, breads, cookies, and even bagels, but he didn't stop there. He liked to experiment with new doughs and toppings. His recipes were not known elsewhere, for they were his own creation. Yes, he was an innovator of sorts, but he never wrote down any of his recipes, so each morsel he created was doomed to die on the tongue as soon as it was swallowed. He never repeated a single one of these experiments, because so many more were ready to burst out of his head. He hummed while he baked and he hummed while he played.

Unfortunately, Elikai felt underappreciated. He went to all that trouble to create unique and tasty treats and no one complimented him. Tales of other Menehune communities, particularly the one in the Thousand Years' Forest, peaked his bubbling curiosity. Maybe they'd appreciate his baked goods.

Because the Menehune worked by night and slept by day, Elikai chose that time of day just before the sun slips out of sight, that time when the others were still asleep to sneak out of Ainahou Forest. He had to be secretive, because it was simply taboo to travel across territory where humans lived. He tied a few essential belongings into a spare loin cloth, put on fresh wrist and ankle bracelets of green fern and *maile*, and started down the path to where he thought he'd avoid human activity. He hummed every step of the way, for he was certainly a most cheerful Menehune.

Soon the trees of Ainahou Forest thinned, and Elikai saw rows of cottages. Just as he was about to alter his path away from these dwellings, he smelled a whiff of baking cookies wafting from an open window. He took in a deep breath. "Macadamia-raisin," he said aloud. As he neared the window, he heard humming, a pleasant enough male voice. The humming ceased as soon as the hummer sensed a presence at the window.

A *kanaka,* a large, muscular Hawaiian, appeared in the cottage doorway. Beneath his white apron, this bare-chested man, wore denim shorts and *slippahs*. His large hands were dusted with flour, and he called out to Elikai as the Menehune attempted to scoot along. "Little man, come closer and tell me where you are going."

Frightened, Elikai realized he had encountered his first human. What to do? Out of caution, he stopped short. He didn't want to ignore the man altogether, for he was curious. But he didn't know if any humans could be trusted. As a Menehune, he just couldn't lie. "I'm going to the Thousand Years' Forest to find those who will appreciate my baking."

"Don't be afraid, little man, I won't hurt you. I'm a baker, too. I simply want to know why you're so interested in my baking."

"I don't mean to offend you, sir, but I caught a whiff of your cookies. Being an experienced baker, I detected something missing from your macadamia-raisin recipe."

"Little man, do you realize I am Kaela, a master baker, the sole baker for this whole village? And you insult my cookies by saying something's missing? That recipe is old, tried, and true, my impertinent little friend. No one has improved on it for many years."

"I can," said Elikai.

"You can what?" asked Kaela. His bare chest gleamed with sweat from the heat of his oven. "You haven't even tasted the cookies."

"I don't have to taste them. I can smell what's wrong with them. I'm sure I can improve on your recipe if you let me try."

"Who will be the judge? Who will compare the two batches?" asked Kaela.

"Why you, yourself, of course," replied Elikai. "Who better than a master baker to be the judge? If you will allow me the ingredients and the use of your oven, plus forty minutes of privacy, I will present my offering for your judgment."

"Privacy?" asked Kaela. Frowning, he scratched the wart that sat on the side of his thick nose.

"Yes, privacy," said Elikai. "Go take a short nap and cool off while I do my magic."

Shaking his head, Kaela left the kitchen and the little Menehune to his purported task. Forty-minutes later, he returned to find Elikai arranging twenty-four cookies on one of Kaela's display plates.

"Here, taste one," said Elikai, delicately holding one out.

Kaela took the cookie and examined both sides of it to determine if it was fully baked. He sniffed at it. Then he broke it in two, listening for a snap. Next, he put one of the halves in his mouth and chewed slowly, never changing his expression. Finally, he swallowed and looked down at his fellow baker. "What did you put in it?"

"What's the matter?" asked Elikai. "Don't you like it?"

"I do, I do," Kaela replied. "It's the most delicious cookie I've ever tasted. I'd like to buy your recipe. Name your price."

"But I don't write anything down," protested Elikai. "I've never had the need to. In fact, I don't know anything about recipes. I don't write my ingredients down. I just do all my baking straight out of my head."

"You have a beautiful product here and I'd like to market it for you." Kaela said, taking two steps forward.

"Thank you, sir." Elikai took one step backward just in case.

"My name is Kaela. I get up at five a.m., six days a week, and deliver my baked goods to the High Grande Food Market. They've been complaining that some of my products are left on the shelf in favor of a new competitor's goods. Perhaps you could help me turn that around."

"Thanks, but I bake purely for pleasure," said Elikai. "The pleasure of kudos and compliments."

"It used to be that way for me, too," said Kaela. "But now I'm all out of fresh ideas. I worry too much, so it isn't fun anymore. That manager has heard my excuses over and over again so many times that he's tired of listening to me. I might even lose my bakery. And that's the only way I have to make a living."

"I'm sorry, but I don't know how I can help you," said Elikai.

"Say, do you have improvement ideas for other baked goods as well as my macadamia-raisin cookies?" asked Kaela.

"I most certainly do," replied Elikai. "I do it all the time."

"What's your name, little man. I think we can help each other." Kaela took another step closer to him.

"I am known as Elikai and I am a Menehune." This time he didn't step away, and Kaela was now within touching distance.

Kaela put his hand on Elikai's tiny shoulder. "What if I can teach you to write down the recipes, so we can reproduce all those wonderful baked goods you create."

"Why do I need recipes? What would I do with all the baked goods that I reproduce? Where would I keep them?"

"Perhaps we could become partners in my bakery. Then I could sell all your delicious goods and everyone would know what a masterful baker you are."

"I have no interest in what humans think about my baking. What do I get out of all this work? I'm not being selfish, but I don't want to be taken unfair advantage of either."

Kaela's gray eyes turned murky as he calculated a new approach. "Elikai, why did you leave your people and come here in the first place?"

"I didn't plan to come here at all," he replied. "I merely started out to find some Menehune who would appreciate my baking."

"Elikai, are you hungry?"

"Now you're talking. I'm always hungry."

"My little friend, do you need a place to sleep while we do all of this baking?"

"I do."

"Then I have the perfect solution," said Kaela. "You will come stay in my home and eat my food while I teach you how to write down your recipes. After you write them down, I can continually bake them for sale at the High Grande market."

"How long do you think it will take to overcome the bakery competition at the market?" asked Elikai.

"Perhaps a month or two," replied Kaela. "Why?"

"I will make a pact with you. For two months and two months only, I will stay with you and bake everything for you under the following conditions. One, I write down no recipes. Two, I work completely alone at night, in secret, and sleep during the day. Three, whatever I bake is yours to keep or sell as long as I am free to leave at the end of my two months' stay. Any profit you make is also yours to keep."

Kaela extended his hand to be shaken. The little guy grabbed Kaela's index finger and shook it up and down twice. They were now partners. Kaela had promised to abide by Elikai's terms.

The Menehune proved to be a quick and clever baker and, within a few nights, he was turning out a steady supply of breads and pastries in a delectable variety. Their partnership blossomed. With amazing speed, Kaela's baked goods became so popular that the sales began to grow as well. Soon they edged the competitor off the shelf. Kaela received more shelf space, and the competitor was given less and less until he was gone. Each morning, Kaela's filled-to-capacity delivery van drove to market. Then deliveries to a neighboring village market became viable. At the end of the first month there were even buyers from markets in surrounding villages trying to place orders. Kaela envisioned going big time. He only needed one more delivery truck to expand his business.

But the agreed-upon two-month pact eventually came to an end. Each of them had benefited enormously. Although Kaela seemed too busy to notice the coming deadline, in reality he intended to ignore it. Elikai planned to leave as soon as he woke up that final evening. Kaela pleaded and pleaded. "Another month, another week, another day, even one written recipe." But the answer was always No.

"A promise is a promise, my friend," said Elikai. "But you don't need me anymore. I left the secret ingredient in a small clear bottle for you." He pointed to it on the work table.

"And what happens when the bottle is empty?" asked Kaela. "My competitor will take over again."

Elikai didn't answer. His head tilted to one side as he perceived a bit of connivance churning in Kaela's brain. The Menehune smelled betrayal as acutely as if it were a pan of fresh-baked taro rolls. Alerted, he bolted for the door as fast as his short legs would carry him. Kaela caught up with him in two giant human steps and scooped Elikai's slight body off the floor in one huge swooping motion.

"Put me down!" Elikai cried. "Please! You agreed to let me leave at the end of two months."

"But I need you to stay and help me become a multi-village business. You're what I've waited for all my life. Just a little longer, my friend," Kaela pleaded once more. "Another month or two."

"No! No! No! Put me down. You're hurting me." He kicked and flailed and struggled with hardly any effect on his captor.

Kaela held him tightly under one arm while he scanned the room for something or some place to contain the little guy until he came around to his way of thinking. Then he spied the three-foot-high bread oven, now cooled after many hours after baking. With his free hand, he flung open the cast-iron door and shoved Elikai inside, depositing him at the rear of the oven. Elikai stood up as fast as he could, ready to leap out again, but Kaela quickly slammed the oven door shut on the little guy. He could hear Elikai's muffled cries coming from inside the tall black appliance.

Elikai shrieked, "Help! Help, let me out of here this instant. You can't hold me prisoner."

"Oh but I can," Kaela replied.

"I'll make a big mess in here if you don't let me out." He kicked hard against the door, but neither the door nor his captor paid any attention to his efforts.

Kaela turned a deaf ear to him, and went to bed thinking the Menehune would be more reasonable in the morning.

Elikai found the darkness creepy and lonely. With tears in his eyes and his little body shivering, he sat down, feeling quite sorry for himself. But soon he began to think more clearly. *The door is held by magnets,* he thought. *I should be able to just push it open.* But when he put his shoulder to the frame it just wouldn't move. He backed up at least a foot-and-a-half and ran at the same spot. The door moved open slightly, but the magnets pulled it back. *Maybe I need just a little more help,* he decided. Searching, searching in the darkness, his eyes rested on the steel racks used to hold the trays for baking.

A resolved Elikai stood and rolled up his sleeves. He lifted one rack out of its slots and dragged it until it leaned against the big cast-iron door—thus lending additional weight for the little man to push it open. *I hope that's all the assistance I'll need,* he thought. He lowered his shoulder and threw his small but muscular body at the steel rack against the oven door. This time not only did the door budge, but it swung wide, sending Elihai flailing through the air and flopping on his stomach in the middle of the workroom.

He picked himself up, swung the door shut again, and started for the front door of the cottage to gain his freedom. But before he reached the outside, he remembered the bottle containing the secret ingredient. He turned back, grabbed it off the work table, and headed for the door once more. Just then, Elikai heard Kaela's footsteps on the staircase. Kaela must have heard the commotion when the helpful rack flopped with a thud to the oven floor.

Kaela made a beeline for the oven to check on his prisoner. The oven was empty. He spun around and saw Elikai standing outside, holding up the mystery bottle so his captor could clearly see it.

"You asked me what would happen when the bottle became empty," said the Menehune. He turned it on its side and poured half the liquid out onto the doorstep. When he righted the bottle, Kaela saw that the bottle was full again. He gasped. "It will never be empty!"

Kaela was so stunned by what he saw that he sank into a chair and moaned. He realized the little guy had provided a way for him to continue producing superior baked goods after all. He regretted what he had done to his little partner. Scrambling to his feet, he rushed after the Menehune, but stopped when he heard a crash. He was too late. Elikai had dropped the bottle on the stone doorstep. The shattered glass shards and liquid had spread over the entire doorstep, making it impossible for the barefoot Kaela to pursue him.

Elikai ran as fast as he could, his little legs whirling like a spinning pinwheel. He disappeared from view and was never seen in the village again. Darting far off onto a trail, he slowed down to a leisurely trot far away from humans and their false promises. Finally, under a full moon, he came upon the Thousand Years' Forest. There he settled in a community of Menehune who loved sweets and breads and appreciated his extraordinary baking.

Kaela's bakery survived, but only in a marginal, scraping-by, way. He often thought of his little partner and the way things might have been.

The Legend of Kilo

Kilo was small, even for a Menehune. If you stretched him out flat next to a ruler, he would barely reach the twelve-inch mark. Oh, but he was the quick one. No one ever saw him on the move. He appeared here and then there and was never seen moving between. Blessed with superior vision, he became an especially fine archer as well. He used his archery skills to capture mullet, ulua, barracuda, perch, eels, and shrimp in the brackish fishponds. Constructed expertly by his fellow Menehune, some of these ponds were least a thousand years old.

Kilo had not yet tested the sheer strength of his newest archery bow. When he crept up to the edge of one particular pond, expecting to spear a silver perch with an arrow, an accident occurred. He inadvertently released the arrow prematurely. It shot into a thicket of reeds that surrounded the pond. Ordinarily, this wouldn't have been a problem, a lost arrow at most. But at this moment he heard an anguished scream erupt from the ultimate destination of the arrow. Had he wounded one of his fellow Menehune? A Menehune is not supposed to do any harm. He felt terrible.

A miserable whining ensued, so a worried Kilo headed off in that direction, brushing the tall grass and reedy plants aside as he plodded through the marshes. When he pushed away the last of the tangled growth, he discovered the soles of two monstrous feet and a massive ōkole (buttocks) with an arrow sticking out of its left cheek. *Oh my gosh! I shot a human straight in his ōkole. Are wounded humans on their bellies dangerous?* He walked around the huge writhing human, giving it plenty of berth. He then saw the human's face, lying on its right side, the white hair, the wrinkles, and weathered skin. Kilo determined that this was an elderly male. The man's left arm flailed, reaching around himself, searching, attempting to find the errant arrow to pull it out, but it was totally beyond his physical reach.

"So sorry," said Kilo. "It was an accident. I didn't mean to shoot you. I didn't even know you were there."

"Sorry, shmorry," the old man bellowed. "Help me get this damn thing out. It hurts like hell."

Darting behind the human again, Kilo gave the arrow a tug, but it wouldn't budge. He tried several other positions, even the over-the-shoulder angle to pull it out, but to no avail. As a last resort, he lay down on his back, fitting his own body on the old man's back, with one foot on each of the man's ōkole cheeks. With both hands, he tried to pull the arrow up. It moved slightly, then suddenly broke free and out with a terrible ripping and snapping sound, accompanied by a major yelp from the old man. The two of them sprawled on the muddy ground for several minutes, exhausted from the struggle.

"Oh!" moaned the old man. "My ōkole is so sore I won't be able to sit down. How am I going to earn a living? I have a wife and three children to feed."

"How does this accident prevent you from earning a living?" asked Kilo.

"I'm a fisherman. Now I won't be able to even sit in a boat or on the end of a pier to ply my catch at the end of a line. And I'm much too old and feeble to stand and cast a seine net anymore."

"Please forgive me," said Kilo. "Since I'm the cause of your miserable situation, perhaps you'll permit me to supply fish for your family until you are fully recovered."

"That's most generous of you, little man," said the fisherman. "Are you, by any chance, a Menehune? I've heard a lot of stories about them, but I never thought I would meet one, especially not this way." The old man struggled to his feet and shook off the excess mud from the front of his jeans and T-shirt.

"Yes, I am a Menehune and I am called Kilo. What may I call you, fisherman?

"I am Akoni," replied the old man, "and I don't hold any grudge against you. I live on the first farm past the intersection up *mauka* way." He pointed toward the mountains.

Akoni extended his hand for a shake, and Kilo took hold of the old man's middle finger and shook it gently.

* * * *

Kilo kept his word. Numerous sizeable ulua, mullet, and other fish appeared on the rear doorstep of the fisherman's home every morning. It was well known that Menehunes sleep by day and work by night, so Kilo would fish the night through and deposit his entire catch there. Akoni's grateful family had plenty to eat and a surplus to sell or trade at the local market for their other necessities. Kilo had set no exacting terms for this arrangement—only that Akoni's *ōkole* heal well enough to resume his occupation as a fisherman.

In fact, at the end of three weeks, Akoni could sit comfortably for an hour or two. He wanted to notify Kilo that he was able to go back to work, but the fisherman's wife, Kamene, had another idea. She wanted Akoni to start working again, but she didn't want Kilo to know about it. She envisioned her husband fishing by day and Kilo fishing by night, but neither seeing the other at the fishponds. She had plans to sell the extra fish, envisioning the additional luxuries they would allow her to purchase at market, and perhaps a little savings for a rainy day, too. Akoni spoke against this sneaky arrangement, for he was an honest man. To keep peace in the family, he surrendered to his wife's wishes. While his family prospered greatly over the next few weeks, he felt depressed over cheating Kilo, but he could do nothing about it.

The Menehune was no fool and began to think the fisherman's recovery was taking a suspiciously long time, so he laid a trap. Sure enough, by staying at the pond beyond sunrise, he spied Akoni with a baited line over the edge of the log pier.

"Akoni, my friend, why have you cheated on our arrangement? Have I not kept my part of the bargain? Is your family wanting for anything?"

Akoni looked crestfallen and mightily embarrassed. "You have been most generous, my little friend. I certainly have no complaint with you."

"Then why have you betrayed me?"

"It is Kamene, my wife, who concocted this farce. I feel helpless to oppose her, for she is greedy and wishes to take advantage of your kindnesses. For myself, I wanted to tell you I could return to work, but she would hear none of it."

"Then take me to your Kamene, and I will see for myself how greedy she is."

Kilo followed Akoni to his farmhouse up the road. Because of his lightning speed he had little trouble keeping up with Akoni's giant human steps. Upon arriving at the old man's home, they found Kamene sunning herself in the backyard.

With fists on his tiny hips, Kilo asked the woman, "Why have you forced your husband to cheat on our arrangement?"

"I have done no such thing," Kamene lied. "It was his idea all along." The moment she uttered this betrayal of her good husband, both her arms turned a silvery green, the color of fish scales.

"I sense that you are lying to me," said Kilo. "It is not permissible to lie to a Menehune."

"What have you done to my arms?" Kamene screamed. "I've done nothing wrong." No sooner had these false words burst from her lips than her legs also turned a slimy, silvery, fish-like green.

Kilo jumped up onto an old tree stump, so he would gain height and a sense of authority. "Ma'am, you want fish so much you might as well become a fish," Kilo intoned.

With fury in her weasely eyes, Kamene looked down on her arms and legs. "So this is *your* doing, you little twerp." She reached out to grab Kilo from his perch, but he vanished from her sight.

He reappeared on the doorstep. Screeching in frustration,

Kamene pursued him there, but again, too late. Gone from the doorstep. Now atop the woodshed. Again her lunging attempt foiled. Kilo led her on a wild "here again-gone again" chase around the yard until she fell flat on her face in exhaustion. At this point an archery bow with arrow appeared in Kilo's hands.

"No, no, spare her!" cried Akoni upon seeing Kilo's intention. He tried to reach out and spoil Kilo's aim, but, quick as lightning, the Menehune had moved to another vantage point and shot the arrow squarely into Kamene's right *ōkole* cheek. She screamed so loud the trees shook.

"Don't worry, my friend," said Kilo. "She will recover nicely from her wound, but the fish scales will remain until she gives up her greedy ways. Goodbye, Akoni. I will see that you always have a favorable catch."

The fisherman never saw Kilo again, but somehow his Menehune friend continued to watch out for him.

The Legend of Amalia

In legends and art, we learn—perhaps not often enough—of female Menehune, worthy ladies and girls who form an integral part of the little-people's society. Amalia was a winsome, chubby lady with a doll-like face, standing only fourteen inches high. Menehune women are believed to be ageless, so who's to say the exact number of her years? In addition to being charming, clever, and kind, Amalia's real claim to fame was her ability to see into the minds of others. She knew when you were telling the truth and when you were not. She knew your intentions before they became actions. And she knew your raw feelings before you became vulnerable.

Be reminded: To avoid human interaction, the Menehune lived in the deep forest, working by night and sleeping by daylight. Their uniquely keen eyesight enabled them to see perfectly in the densest of darkness. At sunset or before daybreak, Amalia collected wildflowers in the forest—always careful not to pluck *ohi'a lehua*. The elders always warned that picking it would bring drenching rain showers and floods.

Amalia's rotund, bouncy figure betrayed her passion for all taro dishes, as well as breadfruit, bananas, and coconut. Her thick coal-black hair fell around her face and flared out, as if caressing and protecting her shoulders. She lived in a house of hard wood and thatch with her parents and two brothers. None of her famiy members would play games with her because they were well aware of her excellent mind-penetrating talents. They never had the pleasure of winning. Thus, she spent her spare time looking for rare and beautiful things in the forest.

The tiny lass had never met a human, but had heard that they were a greedy lot, prone to lying and cheating. During one long night, Amalia had ventured farther than usual from home As the sun prepared to make its appearance, she heard thunderous footsteps and felt the associated vibrations underfoot. As they grew louder and more pronounced, she became frightened. Clutching her basket full of fragrant flowers, she hid behind a broad tree trunk. She knew whatever it was had stopped just the other side of this same tree. Amalia could see the giant shadow cast beside the tree, but she had hardly any notion of what it was. The next thing she heard was a sniffing noise, and then a humongous sneeze that blew all the nearby ground cover in a single direction. *It must be a human,* she thought. *No animal can sneeze like that. And that shadow seems like a much oversized version of my older brother.*

"Damned flowers set off my hay fever again!" boomed the enormous human creature on the other side of the tree.

Amalia shuddered with fear and hugged the tree closely. But the shadow moved away. Now when she looked up, two bulging eyes stared down at her.

"What is this I'm seeing?" the human thundered, hurting Amalia's ears. "Has someone lost a doll here in the middle of the woods?" He started to reach down for her, but she slid farther around the tree trunk. "The little doll moves like it's alive. Am I being tricked?"

"I am not a doll," the little person asserted. "I am a living, breathing Menehune. Are you a human person?"

"Yes, little lady." He bent low, and with two hands, reached around the tree trunk in both directions until he trapped Amalia in between. She trembled with fear as he wrapped the fingers of his right hand about her tiny waist, lifted her straight up, and held her at arm's length to view his prize.

"Why, it's a lovely young lady in miniature," he declared. "A Menehune, you say? Like the little people of the deep forest the *kupuna* (old folks) talk about?"

"Yes, so you'd better let me go before you anger the Menehune gods," she answered. She instantly disliked him. He had angry dark eyes, a straggly brown beard, and snarled hair that looked like it hadn't been washed in many a moon.

"Hah!" he replied. "I am not afraid of the Menehune gods, nor their magic." He tucked her under one arm and took off in a direction away from her home. They traveled more than an hour before arriving at his modest wood-frame house. Once inside, the human set her down on the kitchen table. He wrapped and knotted several turns of string about her tiny legs and anchored the other end around a table leg.

"You're hurting me," she whispered, her cheeks a cascade of tears. "Why are you making a prisoner of me? I've done you no harm, Mr. Human." Amalia continued to shiver with fear, but also distaste as she viewed his rumpled, red-checkered shirt, grimy pants, and high, laced boots.

"I have no wish to harm you, my pretty little one. I am lonely and have no one to play games with. You appear to be the perfect plaything for me. You can start by telling me your name."

She gathered up her courage and began to plan a way to outsmart her captor. *I can use my mind to know what he's thinking.* Aloud she said, "My name is Amalia and I live in the forest with my parents and two brothers."

"A pretty name for a pretty little lady," he responded. "Would you like to play games with me?"

Amalia smiled as she laid out her strategy. "I bet I can guess your name in three tries," she replied, now confident she could get the upper hand. *I'd better not guess it in less than three tries or he will become suspicious of my powers.*

"That's a good one," he answered. "Three tries, hah. Go ahead and try."

146

"Let me see. Is it Keoki?"

"Ha-ha, no!" he boomed.

"Then it must be Heneli," she offered.

"Oh no, little Amalia, you are about to lose your wager. Imagine guessing my name in only three tries."

Amalia kept silent for the next several minutes as though deep in thought. Then she took a long breath and said, "I have it now. It's Palani, isn't it?"

"What?" he gasped. "How did you do that? My name is not that common."

"Just a wild guess," she replied as modestly as she could. "Only a wild guess."

"You like to play games, don't you?" Palani asked.

"Why, yes," she replied. "How could you possibly know that?" she added, hoping to toy with his ego.

"Just a guess," he returned with a smile. "Perhaps you want to play cards with me—gin rummy or poker?" He showed her a deck of cards.

"I don't know how to play those card games," she returned.

"Since you like guessing games, how about Twenty Questions?" he asked.

Now I have him, Amalia thought. *He's suggesting a mind game.* "I don't know that game," she said aloud. "Can you teach me to play this Questions game?"

"Sure," he said. He explained the rules right down to the last detail. They would take turns, asking each other twenty questions about a person, place, or thing written on a piece of paper concealed by the first person. "I'll start by writing something down and hiding it from you. Then you can start guessing what's on my piece of paper. A correct guess wins the game. More than twenty wrong questions or guesses loses the game."

"What does the winner win?" she asked.

"Do you have anything of value—money, possessions, and the like?"

Amalia shook her head, and thought for a moment. "I

know. If I win, you'll let met go home to my family, and we'll part as friends."

"And what if I should win?" asked Palani.

"You'll take the bonds off me, and I will freely stay to entertain you for one week, during which time I promise not to run away."

"Why should I believe that you won't run away?"

Amalia drew up her tiny body in a stance of indignation. "Menehune cannot break promises. It's our way. But how do I know I can trust *you*?"

"You have to trust me, for I presently have the advantage over you. You are already my captive. I assure you that you can do no worse."

"So how about we take turns at guessing in five games apiece. Whoever has guessed right the most times is the winner. My freedom or your obliging guest for a week."

"Make that a month and you have a deal." Palani held out his massive right hand for a shake, and she shook his pinkie up and down three times in agreement.

"A month it is." Amalia shook his pinkie twice more. "Take off my string, and let the games begin."

Palani untied her as agreed. Out of the five games that Amalia did the guessing, she allowed him to win a generous three. Of the other five, just one—just enough wins for him to believe that he was truly competitive. She was in control the entire time, for she could read his mind like it was her own. As the winner of six games to four there was no question who had won the wager.

But will he honor the outcome or not? she wondered. "Now it's time for me go home to my family," she said aloud.

"Another game or two?" he begged.

"I have won my freedom, which you had taken by force, and you have nothing left that I want. So why should I gamble my freedom all over again?"

Palani gazed down at her. "Like I told you, my pretty Amalia, I'm a lonely man. Would you actually come back another time and play games with me? I could teach you all kinds of new games."

148

"I would gladly come back if you could prove to me that all humans are not a greedy lot, prone to lying and cheating. That is what all Menehune think about humans. My family would never let me come back unless you tell me how to prove this true."

"Just by letting you go home to your family should be proof enough," he said. "Don't you think so?"

"Yes, I suppose so," she answered, thinking his scruffy beard wasn't as fierce as she'd first thought.

Palani frowned. "I know you've tricked me somehow, but I can't figure out how you did it."

Amalia chuckled. "Yes, I did, but that is my secret." She trotted to the door. "You enjoyed the games, didn't you? Isn't that what you wanted? I promise I'll come back and play again. For now, I must get home before the sun comes up."

Palani watched as little Amalia disappeared through the door. A lopsided smile appeared on his face. The lonely human had made a new friend.

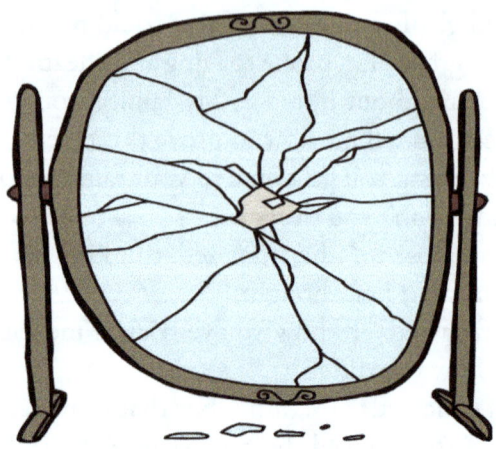

Our Shattered Fairy Tales

Perhaps as authors we sense ahead of time that a story is going to turn out unfavorably and we want to improve upon the ending. At other times, we feel this uncontrollable urge to put our own personal twist on an entire story to make it lighter or funnier or weirder or even put the shoe on the other foot, letting the villain swap places with the victim. It's all fair game for the mind.

The Brothers Grimm created a number of gruesome characters and came up with some pretty grisly plots, and many authors before us have attempted to alter what the brothers started. The exercise may not improve on the original, but it shares the fun in trying. The following stories are our attempt at a few Shattered Fairy Tales.

Wooden It Be Wonderful?

Dr. Harrison Cutter, freshly scrubbed, strode into the operating room. "Nurse, is the patient prepped and ready?"

"Yes, Doctor, he's on the table and under anesthesia. Will he need a sap transfusion?"

The surgeon squinted as he made his decision. "I don't believe so." He took a moment to study the lineup of sterilized tools laid out on the stainless-steel counter. "Okay, Nurse. Looks like we're ready to go. Coping saw!"

She laid the handle of the sharp instrument in his latexed palm with a slap of efficiency, then watched as the surgeon used the thin blade to create intricate shapes.

"Chisel!"

"What size, Doctor?"

"Deep Gouge, Number Six."

"Yes, Doctor!"

After carving out the proboscis profile that the patient had requested, Dr. Cutter demanded, "Shallow Gouge, Number Two!"

"Yes, Doctor!"

An hour later, the appendage emerged at an appropriate length and overall shape.

The patient, Pinocchio Gippetty, was still wearing his pointy yellow cap with its red stripe and green feather. The anesthesia had sunk him into a deep sleep. Despite his precarious circumstances, a wooden smile graced his face, attesting to a pleasant dream in progress.

"Detail knife!"

"Yes, Doctor!" The nurse watched as the surgeon's expert hands created contours until a winsome result began to emerge. Exchanging instruments once more, she saw him deftly remove a slight blemish from the proboscis.

"Sandpaper!"

"What grit, Doctor?"

"Surely, Nurse, you should know by now—380 grit. This is the third time we've done this operation on Mr. Gippetty."

Nurse cringed and murmured, "Yes, Doctor, of course." She handed him the superfine grade of sandpaper and watched while he smoothed over each rough spot.

"Stain!"

"What color, Doctor?"

"Matching his skin color, Nurse! Look at the pigment swatch to be sure."

"Skin tone, of course, Doctor," she whimpered.

Dr. Cutter applied the stain with a sterilized gauze pad and massaged it gently until he achieved the correct hue. With a flourish he wiped away the excess stain. "We'll finish with a fine coat of varnish."

"Yes, Doctor."

An hour later, Dr. Cutter stood back to admire his work and said, "We're done. Send him to the recovery room. But we can't discharge him until the varnish dries. In an hour I'll stop by to confirm that he's ready."

"Yes, Doctor."

"And for the sake of Mr. Pino—whatever his name is, I hope to high heaven it's the last time he'll have to endure this surgery. Come to think of it, I could use a nice glass of pinot noir right now." Dr. Cutter peeled off his latex gloves and marched out.

The floor beneath the operating table was covered in wood chips, long sliced curls, and sawdust—evidence that an extraordinary operation had been performed here today on a celebrity figure.

The nurse and orderly transferred the patient to a gurney and rolled him down the hall to the recovery room.

Pinocchio lay flat on his back for the better part of an hour, waiting for the anesthesia to wear off. When he awoke, his hands immediately went to his face. He quickly realized he had his new nose and, hopefully, a fresh start. He knew, with great certainty, that if he lied again, there would be agonizing consequences. His nose would grow and grow. Again. From miserable experience he recalled all the shameful moments when his nose became the object of giggles, guffaws, whispers, and pointed fingers. If he couldn't suppress his compulsion to lie, he knew that soon he would have difficulty reaching the end of his nose to wipe it. His head's minimal turning radius would be limited; he would be knocking over glassware, teacups—anything in his path. And it was always humiliating when his nose arrived several seconds before he did. Fully awake now, he mused, *The surgeon advised me to see a therapist. Maybe I should.*

* * * *

Pinocchio took the surgeon's advice and made an appointment with Dr. Phillipshead Unscrew, who had a reputation for dealing with Proboscis Prevarication Disorders. At his first session with the therapist, Pinocchio settled uneasily on the brown leather couch and squeezed his eyes shut, fearing what secrets the doctor would uncover.

"So, why are you here?" asked Dr. Unscrew as he stroked his goatee.

Barely above a whisper, Pinocchio said, "I want to stop lying because every time I do, my nose gets longer. It's downright humiliating."

"Just how bad is this nose business?" asked the doctor.

"I've had three expensive operations already. I can't afford any more. I have to cut down, if you'll excuse the expression."

Dr. Unscrew adjusted his horn-rimmed glasses. "Hmm, let

me see. Could it be some trauma from your boyhood, Pinocchio?"

"It could be, Doc. I did a lot of lying back then. But being a mere wooden puppet in the hands of manipulators, how could I be blamed for all that lying? Every time I tried to turn around, there was someone else pulling on my strings."

"So what changed?" probed the good doctor.

"I learned to control my fibbing, and then my outright lies, for a whole year. I was so successful at it that some magical lady from who-knows-where turned my former rigid wooden self into a real-life, flesh-and-blood boy. That is, all but my nose. The lady goofed. My nose remained cursed white oak."

"And how did you feel about that?" asked the doctor.

Pinocchio's voice turned shrill. "I thought it was grotesquely unfair. Other people lie and get away with no visible evidence. Why should my nose give me away so publicly? I have to measure every word that comes out of my mouth. I can't even tell a tiny fib. I have to take the blame for anything I do wrong."

"I see," said Dr. Unscrew, twisting his head away from the clock on the wall. "And just who do you tell these lies to?"

"That's the problem. Anybody who'll listen. The lies just pop out of my mouth, beyond my control."

"You have friends, don't you?" asked the doctor, digging deeper.

"You gotta be kidding, Doc. I don't have any friends. Just a few bad acquaintances. They always got me into trouble. My daddy, the woodcutter, died years ago. Oh, I did have one friend, if you can call him that. His name was Jiminy Cricket. The creepy little guy was always hovering over me, bugging me about right and wrong. I actually liked him, but he was literally in my ear most of the time."

"So what happened to this Mr. Cricket?" asked Dr. Unscrew.

"That's the awful part, Doc. One of my real bad acquaintances stepped on him and flattened him—permanently," replied Pinocchio with a sob in his scratchy voice and a giant tear in his left eye.

"Sorry about that," said Dr. Unscrew, handing his patient a tissue. "What about any relationships with the opposite sex? I'm sure there must have been a female or two in your life, someone who mattered to you."

"Nope. No, wait! I remember a girl, a beautiful girl, who dressed like a princess. Her friends called her Thumbelina." He sighed and his little chest heaved with despair. "She was a tiny thing, only this high." Pinocchio stretched his thumb and index finger to indicate about three inches. A second tear rolled down his cheek, puddling on the couch cushion.

"This sounds promising," declared Dr. Unscrew, now on the edge of his chair. "So what happened? Why didn't friendship bloom?"

"Well, for one thing, she claimed I was always talking down to her. How could I help it, the gal was only three inches high? Besides, she always had this 'I-just-came-in-from-the-garden' smell about her. Then there were her friends. The little lady actually hung out with elements of the underworld—mice and moles. Ugh! Our so-called friendship was never destined to be more than a splintered affair."

"I see," said Dr. Unscrew, backing off in disappointment. "And that was all?"

"Not quite. I even looked up a matchmaker once," said Pinocchio.

"And how did that turn out?" asked Dr. Unscrew.

"After twenty minutes I discovered he wasn't a Matchmaker, the kind who pairs people up. Not at all. He wanted to know how many ignitable matches he could make out of my nose. He was a matchstick maker! You better believe I got out of *there* in a hurry."

"Such a shame. An understandable mistake," offered the doctor.

"So, Doc, how do I stop lying?"

Dr. Unscrew stood. He helped Pinocchio up to a sitting position, and turned to the white cabinet on the wall. Opening the glass door, he removed a small medicine bottle full of white capsules and handed it to Pinocchio. "Whenever you feel the need to lie, excuse yourself and take one of these pills. It will keep you from actually lying. Come back when you need more."

"Gee, thanks, Doc," said Pinocchio, bouncing up from the couch. "I'll see you in a few months."

* * * *

Three months passed quickly. Pinocchio returned to the therapist for more pills. "Hey, Doc, these pills are great. I haven't lied even once!"

Dr. Unscrew handed him a refill, along with this advice: "By the time you consume these pills, you will no longer need them to keep from lying."

As Pinocchio left the office, Dr. Unscrew smiled, extremely pleased with himself. He had prescribed a placebo—sugar-filled cap-sules—to cure another case of Proboscis Prevarication Disorder.

Schloffin Beauty

**"Schloffin" is an absurdly loose translation
of the Yiddish word "sleep" or "sleeping."**

Aurora Schloffin wasn't a real princess. She was actually the pampered teenage daughter of indulgent, well-to-do Jewish parents. After graduating from high school, the young lady wiled away most of her days on the living room sofa, consuming chocolates and watching soap operas on TV with her many friends. Oh, not so many chocolates as to misshape her voluptuous figure, for she desired to remain beautiful at all costs. She also took pride in her raven-black tresses and the delicate freckles sprinkled across her peachy complexion.

Such was the life of Aurora. That is, until her mother took sick and died. Thirteen months later her lonely father, Abel Schloffin, remarried. His bride, Minerva Maleficent, chose to keep her maiden name and not become Minerva Maleficent-Schloffin, simply because she didn't believe in hyphenated names. Abel adored her and naively never noticed that his new wife was insanely jealous of his only child. But Aurora saw right through the evil woman and her mean ways. The two fought incessantly, and most of these clashes ended with a resounding slap on her stepdaughter's face.

Aurora was no longer a princess. Her days on the living room couch were over. She was forced to do Minerva's chores, even scrubbing floors. But that wasn't all. Minerva forced her to take a job—as pickle slicer behind the counter at Izzy Hullamoizer's Deli. Even worse, Aurora had to turn over her paycheck to Minerva every payday. Aurora protested, but to no avail.

After weeks of helplessly submitting, one day she stood her ground and refused to relinquish her paycheck. Her refusal unleashed Minerva's fury as never before. She lunged toward her stepdaughter with a roundhouse slap that sent Aurora flying. The poor girl's head slammed against a door jamb, causing her to collapse on the floor in a coma.

Months dragged by. Abel, distraught and visibly aged, visited his comatose daughter daily in the hospital. In despair, he brought her home with all the elaborate life-sustaining medical equipment she required—and charged Minerva Maleficent with Aurora's care and maintenance.

The tables had turned. Grudgingly, Minerva now had to wait on her stepdaughter hand and foot and everything in between. She tolerated the arrangement because she truly believed that neither Abel nor Aurora would be around much longer. Then she would inherit all of the considerable Schloffin fortune. When she had a moment to herself, Minerva sat beside Aurora's bedside and watched TV. That is, until the TV shut down altogether of its own accord. When Hy (short for Hyman) Definition, the TV serviceman, arrived, Minerva retreated to her own room, leaving him to his full technician's skills.

Well, when Hy saw Aurora for the first time, as she lay there in her teddy negligee on the silk sheets, he fell instantly and deeply in love.

Abel saw the repairman mooning over Aurora and told him, "Fix the TV, Mr. Repairman, and keep your eyes where they belong."

Hy repaired the TV and then dared to look across the room once more. He was so enraptured with the Schloffin beauty that he bent over and gave Aurora a kiss. Not the explosive kiss of lustful passion, mind you, but the long, sincere kiss of lingering and powerful love—enough to last a lifetime. This precious kiss traveled down through the thick, resisting layers of coma and caused Aurora's brain to stir. Soon all her neurons began dancing with glee. Her lips responded first, and then her eyes fluttered open to see her lover. Joyfully, she sat up and hugged him.

"Your TV is all fixed, good as new," Hy told Abel. "And your Aurora, if you'll excuse the expression, is fixed, too. Now that she's awake, may I have your daughter's hand in marriage?" he asked.

"Please, Daddy," pleaded Aurora. "I'd love to be Aurora Definition."

Abel seriously thought about this. *The TV works well now. It might also be nice to have a TV repairman in the family. I could save a lot on my repair bills. And, of course, my dear Aurora is awake and happy.* "Yes, you may have my daughter's hand in marriage," he said.

Minerva was flabbergasted. She wanted no part of this proposal. "Just pay the repair man and send him on his way," she said. But no one listened to her objections, and the glorious wedding took place. What took place in the bedroom on the wedding night was nobody's business, but nine months later, Aurora delivered a healthy set of twins. The ecstatic couple named them Herman and Hermione. Immediately, Aurora's father visited his attorney and altered the terms of his will.

Abel's wife seethed. Minerva Maleficent realized that she now had been relegated to fourth in line for Abel's inheritance—that is, if he left her anything at all. She had to do something about the infant twins or she would remain poor for the rest of her life. Consorting with the cook, she devised a plan. He was to boil the twins in a pot of matzoh ball soup and serve them, sliced in gravy, to the family.

Hy and Aurora assumed Minerva had fed the twins in the kitchen earlier. As it turned out, Moishe the cook was not the malicious person Minerva thought he was. He had secretly sent the twins to a neighbor's house and substituted a baby goat in the soup instead. All through dinner Minerva praised the cook for so fine a meal. Abel didn't think it was so special. But his wife firmly believed they were eating his grandkids instead of just the kid Moishe had provided.

Moishe cooked up one more heroic act. He told Aurora and Hy Definition of the sinister plot Minerva had planned. After retrieving Herman and Hermione from the neighbor's house, Moishe set them down next to Aurora. Joyfully, she hugged her husband and children. Once more all her neurons began dancing with glee. Then husband and wife, holding their twins, danced in a circle, a happy frolic called the *hora*.

Hearing the celebration, Minerva Maleficent burst into the room to find the twins still alive. Minerva screamed like a banshee and flung herself, snarling, at the babies. Hy pulled her away just in time and threw her on the floor.

Just then Abel returned home from work and discovered the evil of his wife's ways. He divorced Minerva, leaving her without a penny to her name, and found himself a new wife—kind, loving, and attentive, who also liked to babysit.

To scrape together a living, Minerva Maleficent had to take over the job as pickle slicer at Izzy Hullamoizer's Deli. She was doomed to cutting her fingers at least once a day.

Aurora and Hy enjoyed married life. He kept his job servicing televisions—and maintained his dear wife so robustly that they lived happily ever after with their twelve children.

Rapunzel Rapaporte

Deep in the quaint little village of Brooklyn Down East stood a nine-story walk-up apartment house. Yes, it's hard to believe—not even one lousy elevator. Rapunzel Rapaporte lived alone on the very top floor. Why? Because the rent was zilch. Do you think a lazy owner or rental agent would climb that many stairs to collect rent or even verify an eviction notice? So Rapunzel lived rent free. The *zaftig* twenty-two-year-old with a round face and plump body felt safe there, too. You know why—the formidable stairs.

Rapunzel had extremely long hair, ninety feet of tresses. She found the length and strength of them quite useful in picking up groceries, mail, and packages from the ground floor. A sturdy wicker basket tied to the tail end of her tresses served nicely. All she had to do was lower and raise it. How did she manage this unorthodox arrangement? A handsome young man in apartment 103 took care of the basket end of all these items. Why? Lester Prince had caught a glimpse of her when she moved in and immediately fell in love with her—so deeply that he agreed to help her survive this way.

Usually the young couple met on the fifth-floor landing for lunch. Lester would walk up carrying the bottle of Manischewitz wine, and Rapunzel would climb down four flights, hauling the

hummus and crackers, a bowl of fresh-cut fruit, and *rugelach* pastries for dessert. She would also bring the tablecloth, paper plates, and plasticware for a complete indoor picnic on the landing. The young couple would sit for hours schmoozing, billing and cooing.

Rapunzel frequently used a gentle rinse to keep her tresses gorgeous. But soon she began noticing something worrisome. Her soft, luxurious hair had started to show an ever-increasing silvery color. It was becoming more unmanageable, too. She was born with light-brown hair just like "Jeanie" of song, so what was causing this ominous situation? She suspected that the color change and stiffness came from the new hair rinse that always arrived in two-gallon jugs. Each monthly coloring took two jugs of full-strength rinse. Momma Rapaporte always sent them over, but the last time they had come in jugs of a slightly different shape and a vaguely different color liquid.

When Rapunzel's silvery hair began to stiffen to an almost metallic texture, it was too hard to brush and difficult to maneuver through the apartment window. And each time she turned around in the apartment, she broke another piece of furniture. So the young woman began to take a closer look at the rinse. She poured it into a shallow bowl to examine it. She saw a light-blue color in the bowl, but then she remembered that the original rinse was a pale green. Now she was really suspicious.

"Who could have meddled with my mix?" she mewed. "Who botched my blend?" she bellowed. "Who fiddled with my fusion?" she fretted. "Only Lester, Momma, and the mailman know I'm living up here."

For answers to her dilemma we have to look back a few months when Momma, the widow Rapaporte, remarried—a *schlemiel* named Bertrum Rumpelstiltskin. Momma chose to keep her last name because of her daughter's wishes. Rapunzel didn't like the man, and Rumpelstiltskin didn't play right at all with *her* name. "Momma, can you imagine anyone walking around with the moniker Rapunzel Rumpelstiltskin?"

Bertrum was a portly man with such a facial tic that it made you think there was a battle going on inside his right cheek. He always took great care to be good to Momma, so she had difficulty see-ing through his conniving ways. Behind her back, he was a sneaky, sleazy, sneering sort. The real reason he married Momma was to get at Rapunzel's hair. Bert wanted to turn her hair into actual silver. He planned to cut the silver locks into manageable lengths, and then mint the lengths into spendable coinage that would make him a for-tune.

Rapunzel saw right through the man and, in her mind, quick-ly labeled him Bad Bert, the wicked stepfather. She was right! For the second time, Bad Bert had replaced her normal color rinse with his perilous silver hair rinse. Momma had no idea what a terrible concoc-tion she was sending over to her daughter.

A few days later, while Rapunzel waited for Lester Prince to come and attach his basket to the tips of her locks, Bad Bert snuck up behind her and tried to cut her hair. But his foot-long scissors just wasn't up to the job.

Bad Bert was undaunted. Snickering, he said to himself, *That new batch of silver rinse is doing its job. Now her hair will become so solid and heavy by morning that she won't be able to move. I'll have no trouble cutting it. All I'll need is a bigger pair of shears. I'm so clever!*

Bad Bert rushed to the local hardware store to purchase a pair of larger, stronger metal shears. By a strange quirk of coinci-dence, the clerk just happened to be none other than Lester Prince. Yes, the same Lester Prince who befriended Rapunzel. He recognized Bad Bert and tried to dissuade him from buying the shears.

"I'm afraid you'll have to fill out this fifty-page form and go through a background check before I can sell you those shears," Les-ter told him.

"What?" cried Bert. "I can buy a gun, a knife, or even a weap-on of mass destruction with less trouble."

"Sorry, those are the rules," said Lester.

"Would a thousand bucks bend those rules some?" asked Bert with a snide, snarky smile.

Lester thought long and hard about this offer. On the one hand, a thousand bucks would go a long way toward buying all those action-video and virtual-reality games he wanted. On the other hand, he would dearly miss those fifth-floor *tête-à-têtes* with Rapunzel. On the third hand...stop...he only had two hands. He assumed he could save Rapunzel later on. Besides, he had scruples hidden somewhere, but didn't know where they were. So he caved to Bert.

"Yeah!" he replied. "I can do that."

"Swell," said Bert. "I knew I could count on you." He began writing a check to Lester.

"Do you want that gift-wrapped?" asked Lester.

"A plain bag will do."

"Paper or plastic?"

"Plastic, of course," said Bert, snickering again. "It's far more destructive, especially in the oceans."

With the transaction completed, Bert left the store. He had far more sinister deeds to get into.

As for Lester, he felt guilty for the rest of his workday.

* * * *

Bad Bert had his devious plans all worked out. Later that day, he rented a helicopter and landed on Rapunzel's roof. With the shears in hand, he snuck down to her apartment and found her fast asleep. So he began his snipping and slicing, then *shlepping* to the helicopter. Now, ninety feet of snipping and slicing and shlepping took some time, so he didn't finish until evening. By then, Rapunzel had risen from her nap and looked in the mirror.

"Goodness gracious!" she cried. "Where has all my silver hair gone? I've been scalped! How will I ever get my groceries now?"

Meanwhile, Lester arrived home from work and started up the stairs carrying at least thirty pounds of pure guilt in his heart. He wanted to reach Rapunzel before Bad Bert started carrying out his nefarious plan. The young man huffed and puffed as he climbed to each landing. It took him over an hour. *Have I made it in time?* he wondered. He burst through the door just as Rapunzel was standing before the mirror. Her would-be rescuer stopped in his tracks.

"You're a bit bald, babe," he babbled. "I've come too late."

"Bad Bert stole my locks," she blurted out.

Just then they both heard the whine of the helicopter blade whirling up to speed on the roof above. The two of them raced out the door and up to the roof in time to see Bad Bert's helicopter struggle to rise a few paltry feet. It lurched forward, then fell out of sight beyond the building. The weight of the silver hair was just too much for the rented chopper, so it took a nosedive into the empty street below. Bad Bert Rumpelstiltskin was no more.

There's a silver lining to this story. Rapunzel reclaimed her clipped silver tresses from the helicopter debris, sold them, and became quite rich, as silver was currently selling at a market high.

Because Lester still loved her despite her baldness, she moved into apartment 103 with him. Her soft, light-brown hair grew back in a few months and now she wore it in curls caressing her shoulders. She had no need to keep it long anymore. They got married and lived happily ever after. And Rapunzel had her Prince—including his last name.

Dot and Her Bot
(Her Puss-in-Boots Robot)

There once was a wealthy widower who lived in a magnificent mansion surrounded by lovely lands. Nothing about this man could be called ordinary. Maximum Delight owned every possession most anybody could ask for—a prestigious financial portfolio, toys and gadgets galore, a collection of antique cars, and money by the bagful. To his credit, his most precious possessions were his clever children—two sons and a daughter, Dorothy Delight, whom he tenderly called Dot. She bore a striking resemblance to her dear departed mother: a dumpling of a girl with carrot-red hair, green eyes, and a shower of freckles sprinkled over her pale cheeks.

At the ripe old age of eighty-nine, Maximum's life drew to a close. To his elder son, Alfred, he left the fabulous mansion, all his lands, and his lucrative portfolio of stocks and bonds. To his younger son, Lee, he left all his toys and gadgets, cars, and cash.

His daughter, Dot, asked, "Is there nothing at all left for me?" There was, but not what she had hoped for. All she inherited from her father was a black rectangular box tied with a white ribbon.

Anguished and humiliated, Dot couldn't imagine what was in the box that could possibly compare with the wealth that her brothers had inherited. She struggled to make sense of it. *Maybe it's something precious—or maybe it's nothing at all.* Hefting the black box and shaking it revealed nothing. Trembling, she pulled the white ribbon free and lifted the cover off.

Disappointment rolled over her as she stared at the contents. A doll. A boy doll, no less. A mere one foot tall, he wore knee-high brown boots with curled toes, a red suit and green cape, and a jaunty feathered hat. He held a tiny sword in his left paw. Yes, paw. Dot lifted the doll out of the box and stood it upright on a table to examine it more closely. *It's a Puss-in-Boots doll,* she reasoned, *but how is this an equitable inheritance?* When she tapped its cat face, it clinked like metal, possibly tin. Another tap caused its whiskers to flicker and its almond eyes to pop alive, bright and alert. Suddenly, it began to move—every limb, joint, and body part. From the way it moved, this was one fine robot.

Dorothy couldn't hide her distress on receiving nothing from her father but a robot doll. But her resentment turned to amazement when it actually began to speak.

"What is your wish, my dear? Tell me and it shall be yours."

"Mr. Puss, I wish..."

"Wait! You may call me Bot for short. I don't like being called Puss."

"Sure, Bot. Now may I have my wish?" asked Dot.

"Of course," he replied.

"The royal family is coming to visit our rural province, and I would like to marry his highness, Prince Prominence. You know, be his willing wife, and live in a cutesy castle with all the royal benefits for the rest of my very, very long life."

"That's asking for quite a bit in one wish," declared Bot.

"A royal union, schmaltzy love, and possibly a spiffy carriage is what I want, so that's what I'll wish for," said Dorothy. "Is that too much to ask?"

"Don't know," said Bot. "I'll see what I can do." Her clever new friend didn't tell her that he had already done some secret exploring. He knew that Alfred Delight was away on a long business trip, and being a trusting sort of guy, had left the magnificent mansion empty with the front door unlocked. He had also assured Dot she could continue to live there in her own bedroom until he returned home.

So Bot trotted on his furry legs down to the Itching Post Tavern, where he waited for the royal family to check in. King Providence, Queen Eminence, and Prince Prominence the Knight arrived with grand fanfare. They were astonished to be greeted by a Puss-in-Boots robot. Waving his sword in one paw, he welcomed them and suggested that the royal family nix the tavern and, instead, stay in luxury at Alfred Delight's mansion.

To add to their comfort, Bot ditched the royal carriage so they could travel in Lee Delight's long white limo through the family lands.

"Whom do we thank for this excellent conveyance and these elegant accommodations?" asked the king and queen in concert.

"Dame Dorothy Delight, Duchess of Wealthland," said Bot, with the skill of an accomplished liar. "She rules the duchy now. Her father, the Duke Maximum Delight, is dead." The Puss-in-Boots robot bowed to the floor, sweeping his feathered cap with a flourish.

"How can we ever repay the duchess for all her kindness?" asked the king and queen.

"Your Majesties, the duchess has but one request," replied the robot in boots.

"Whatever she wants is hers, nothing less," returned the grateful king. "Do tell us what she wants."

"In the morning, Sire and Madam, I'll reveal her request." Bot bowed to the floor, once again sweeping his feathered cap with a flourish.

The next morning, after a lavish breakfast, their son left the formal dining room. Prince Prominence the Knight wandered the chambers, admiring the paintings of ancestors on the walls. While roaming the halls, he had the luck to come across a wide-open door. Within, he saw Dot's image in a gold-framed mirror. He was instantly captivated by her beautiful reflection: her glossy, carrot-red hair with curly bangs covering her high forehead and her luxurious ponytail tied with a bow. He stepped into the room, bowed to Dot, and received a proper curtsy in return.

"Are you Dame Dorothy Delight, Duchess of Wealthland?" asked the Prince. "Or not?"

"Not, I'm afraid. I'm simply commoner Dorothy Delight, known as Dot, and neither a duchess nor a titled dame am I," she said, zipping up her sweat jacket and sliding into her sneakers. "The grand wealth around us belongs to my brothers, Alfred and Lee. You see, all I inherited was a box containing a brilliant little robot."

But Prince Prominence the Knight didn't care. He placed her sweet, inviting arm in his, and they wandered into the lush garden, strolling among poppies, tulips, roses, and irises. On and on they walked, ignoring time. The farther they went, the more they bonded. Somewhere between dusk and dawn the two grew passionately fond of each other. They declared their lasting love near the start of daylight.

But what would the royal couple say when they heard of their son's choice of a bride? Would they allow the two young lovers to marry? Most likely not. The queen shook her finger at her son. "Coupling a royal and a commoner just isn't done. So there!"

Overhearing her fate, Dot took her dilemma to Bot, who purred, "Worry not, my dear. I'll make things right with the king and queen."

So Bot, the Puss-in-Boots, approached their Royal Highnesses to petition them for the two lovers. He explained that Prince Prominence and commoner Dot needed their royal permission to marry.

The king bellowed and roared, and the vexed queen fumed when they heard the word "marry." They responded in concert. "Our son, Prince Prominence, would be better off remaining a bachelor!"

But Bot, the feline robot in brown boots and feathered cap, reminded the king and queen of their royal promise to him: that they would grant Dorothy Delight's petition "for whatever she wants, nothing less." He swayed the royal couple with the fact that it was now the prince's wish as well. "What better reason is there than that? Besides, wouldn't you like a royal grandbaby or two?"

Such exquisite reasoning expelled the anger of the king and queen, and they relented. After all, the royal word had to be as good as gold when granting a petition. And the prospect of royal babies sealed the deal. Bot got his wish and Dot got hers. The marriage made Dot a princess, who became Princess Dorothy, much more appropriate than "Dot" after tying the royal knot.

Prominence and Dorothy lived happily ever after in a charming little castle all their own. They were so grateful to Bot that he became a frequent guest. They always welcomed him with a large bowl of Meow Mix.

And that's the whole story, except for one thought. Who's to say who received the better inheritance—Alf, Lee, or Dorothy? Of course, *we* know, don't we?

ALSO BY ROSEMARY AND LARRY

The Paco and Molly Mystery Series (#1)

Locks and Cream Cheese—In scandal-ridden Black Rain Corners, a Chesapeake Bay mansion harbors locked rooms and deadly secrets. A wily detective and a gourmet cook tackle the case.

The Paco and Molly Mystery Series (#2)

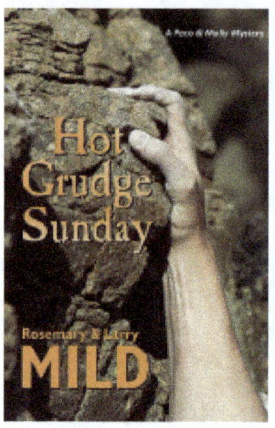

Hot Grudge Sunday—Bank robbers and conspirators derail the sleuths' blissful honeymoon at the Grand Canyon. Can they nail the suspects after they themselves become targets?

The Paco and Molly Mystery Series (#3)

Boston Scream Pie—A teenage girl's nightmare triggers a sinister tale of twins, two feuding families, and a blonde bombshell who hates being called "Mom."

Available on Amazon.com and all e-readers.

The Dan and Rivka Sherman Mystery Series (#1)

Death Goes Postal—Rare 15th-century typesetting artifacts journey through time, leaving a horrifying imprint in their wake. Dan and Rivka risk life and limb to locate the treasures and unmask the murderer. Not quite what they expected when they bought The Olde Victorian Bookstore. (**Also available as an Amazon Audible Audiobook**.)

The Dan and Rivka Sherman Mystery Series (#2)

Death Takes A Mistress—A young Englishwoman is murdered by her lover. Years later, her daughter, seeking revenge, journeys from London to Annapolis, MD to find the killer and her father. But to which family does he belong? Dan and Rivka set out to expose the true villain.

The Dan and Rivka Sherman Mystery Series (#3)

Death Steals A Holy Book—Dan and Rivka inherit a rare Yiddish translation of a 14th-century holy book, but it is stolen and their book restorer is murdered. Can they recover the book and nail the culprit?

Available on Amazon.com and all e-readers.

The Dan and Rivka Sherman Mystery Series (#4)

Death Rules the Night—Dan wants to know why all copies of an important book are missing, not only from the bookstore, but also from all the local libraries and the author's bookshelves. Who is trying to hide the book's secrets and what are they? Can stalking, threats, and even murder sway Dan from solving this mystery? Rivka fears for their lives.

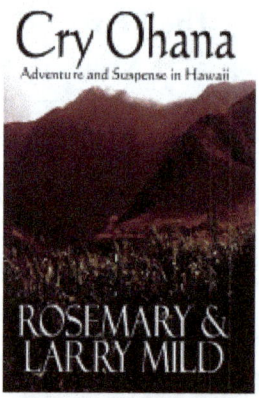

Cry Ohana, Adventure and Suspense in Hawaii—A car accident, blackmail, and murder tear apart a Hawaiian ʻohana (family). Kekoa, the teenage son, witnesses the murder and is forced into life on the run. Danger erupts at a Filipino wedding, a Maui resort, and the Big Island's volcanic steam vents. Can the family re-unite and bring down the killer?

Honolulu Heat—Leilani and Alex Wong anguish over son Noah, an idealistic teenager who teeters on both sides of the law. He meets Nina, his dream girl, but they unwittingly share horrific secrets. Noah finds himself immersed in a bloody feud between a Chinatown protection racketeer and a crimeland don who, ironically, is Nina's father.

Available on Amazon.com and all e-readers.

Murder, Fantasy, and Weird Tales

—Delve into tales of the brave, the foolhardy, and the wicked on their journeys to the unknown in Hawai'i, Japan, Cambodia, Italy, and elsewhere. Art lovers, hit women, a vampire, a lively hologram, and others reveal their secret compulsions.

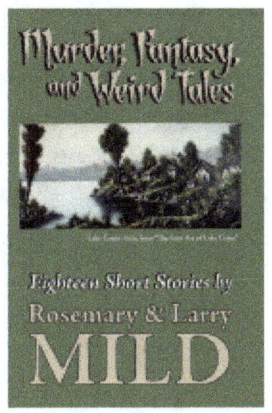

The Misadventures of Slim O. Wittz, Soft-Boiled Detective—"If

you're looking for a truly bumbling gumshoe, you want me, Slim. I'm frequently behind the eight ball and seldom paid. In eight complete mystery stories I always bump into criminals. And you're right: my case record is remarkably shaky."

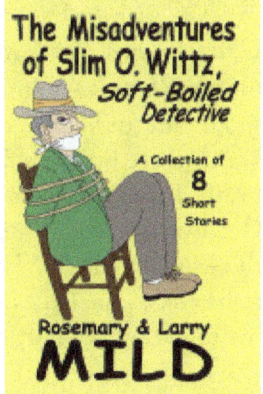

Copper and Goldie • 13 Tails of Adventure and Suspense in Hawaii

—Sam, a disabled ex-cop-turned PI, and his canine sidekick, Goldie, ply the streets of Honolulu in a Checker Cab, looking for fares and solving crimes.

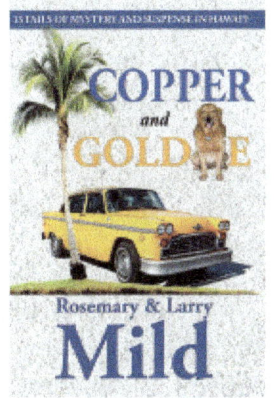

Available on Amazon.com and all e-readers.

Unto the Third Generation—Two young people, each unaware of the other, volunteer to become cryonauts—physically frozen in a life-suspension experiment. Leonard, a steel worker, and Francine, a waitress, postpone their destinies for untold generations. But their lives are in jeopardy —depending upon two world-shaking events.

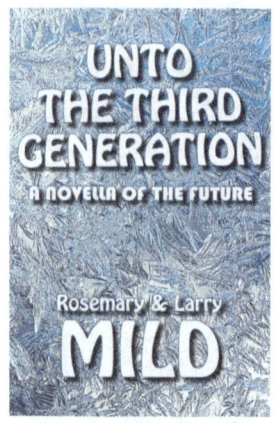

Charley and the Magic Jug and Other Stories—Climb the mountain to the secret cave with Charley. Watch three brothers face a sweet but certain death. Learn how a tiny pill can changes lives. Get away through time with thieves. See what the winds reveal in "Tsunami!" Follow Casey as he chases the ladies. And witness much more, including quirky fairy tales.

Also by Larry

No Place To Be But Here—It is not only Larry's own story, but that of his family. Join him as he tells how his two wives, three children, and five grandchildren have shaped his life as much as he has molded theirs. Tragedy is certainly no stranger as he deals with death, cancer, murder, and global terrorism, not only on the written page, but in his own life.

Available on Amazon.com and all e-readers.

Miriam's World—and Mine
—Miriam Luby Wolfe, a junior at Syracuse U., spent her fall semester in London exploring her talents: singing, dancing, acting, and writing. But she never made it home. A terrorist bomb destroyed her plane over Lockerbie, Scotland. Learn about Miriam, the Pan Am families, the bombers, and the political fallout.

Love! Laugh! Panic! Life with My Mother—Don't we all have mixed emotions about our mothers? Rosemary Mild's mom was super-achieving, but tough to live with. Luby Pollack was a journalist, popular book author, and psychiatrist's wife. Always the heroine, and sometimes the villain, from the viewpoint of her loving but ornery daughter.

In My Next Life I'll Get It Right—
is a collection of personal essays ranging from the hilarious to the serious—keen, sometimes wicked, observations on everyday life. And… wishful thinking mixed with tough reality, See how Rosemary views her two marriages, the good and the not so good. Join her as she takes on sailing, skating, Jazzercise, football, and more—and feel for a mother's heart-wrenching loss.

Available on Amazon.com and all e-readers.

Photograph by Craig Herndon

Larry grew up in New Haven, Connecticut and served in the U.S. Navy during the Korean War. After earning a BS in Information Systems Management from American U. he became a field engineer riding Navy ships for RCA. He spent most of his career at Honeywell/Alliant Techsystems, designing electronic equipment for the U.S. Government. Larry feels fortunate to have wed two terrific ladies. Losing Hannah to leukemia in 1986, he married Rosemary some time later. Together they launched their career coauthoring mystery, suspense, and fantasy fiction in their Honolulu condo overlooking the Pacific Ocean.

Rosemary, a Smith College graduate and former *Harper's* assistant editor, also writes personal essays, many published in the *Washington Post, Baltimore Sun, Chess Life*, and elsewhere. She was divorced when she met Larry on a blind date. He told her, "When I retire, I'm going to write a novel and I want you to help me." She knew he was Mr. Right, so she chirped, "Okay!" Twenty books later, Larry still conjures up their mysterious plots while Rosemary adds the pizzazz. And they haven't killed each other yet!

Email the Milds at: roselarry@magicile.com
Visit them at www.magicile.com